UNDER YOUR SKIN

MATTHEW STANDIFORD

For my wife,

you wouldn't let me give up

—ONE—

Brandon stared up at the wooden beams running across the top of his mother's basement and sighed. Cracks ran through the concrete walls of the house's foundation, chipping the gray paint, and he was sure the chilly air that seeped in through those walls were responsible for the perpetual aches in his bones. He rolled off the bed and went to the small, rectangular windows with the splintering frames and looked out at the front street from his place below the ground. The street was empty, much like his life.

"Brandon, come take your medicine," his mother's nasally voice creeped down through the floorboards and set his teeth on edge. He turned from the window and tried to ignore the constant background hum of the running dehumidifier as it fought its daily battle to keep the dampness at bay. He hated his mother's basement but where were he and Jennifer supposed to go? Beggars couldn't be choosers.

His mind went back to the fire not for the first time. It had burned through their apartment while he was working the night shift at the plant and while Jennifer had escaped with her life it had left her severely scarred. He should have been home instead of picking up shifts. It's not like they had needed the money. He routinely thought about how things would have been different had he been home. He could have gotten her out faster, or the fire wouldn't have happened in the first place. The fire changed everything. Jennifer had been vivacious and beautiful. Now her sullenness seeped into the basement much like the chilly air and water did through the cracks in the floor. He couldn't remember the last time she had gone outside. He remembered how they used to sit on the balcony of their apartment late at night and watch the stars with a clear view of Orion's belt and a bottle of wine. She would smile as the cool breeze blew through her strawberry blonde hair sending it across her face. He couldn't remember the last time he had seen her smile either. Now she sat in the makeshift basement apartment and watched television all day while the guilt ate through him like a cancer. He couldn't understand what she was going through but he could empathize. He didn't think he would want to go outside either if it was his body covered in twisted stretches of burned flesh.

Still, he didn't want her to waste away in the basement. It felt like a crime for something so beautiful to stay inside and wither away in the damp darkness. It was as if he had the rarest flower in the world and instead of letting it bask in the sun for its beauty to be enjoyed by all he took it and locked it away in the dark.

"I'll be there in a minute," he called upstairs as he knelt in front of the recliner Jennifer never left anymore and took one of her scarred hands in his.

"Why don't you get some sun today? It will do wonders for your complexion. The fence is high enough no one should be able to see you in the backyard," he said, trying again. Brandon knew he would never stop trying. Partly because he believed getting out would do her some good and partly because maybe if she stopped hiding away she could move past what happened and then the guilt could give him a rest. She looked at him and his world went cold under her stare.

"Do you want the neighbors to see me like this? Are you trying to humiliate me?" She slurred through the mangled flesh around her mouth.

"Of course not. I love you," he said and she laughed at him. It was devoid of joy and it made his skin crawl.

"Listen to your mommy and take your medicine," she mocked him.

"Come on. Don't be like this," he tried to win her over with a smile but she turned her attention from him and back to the television. She hadn't been interested in seeing anything his way for a long time now. While the fire hadn't claimed her life it had claimed their relationship. Their love had withered and died much like leaves on a tree when the warm summer gives way to fall's cold embrace. Loving her now was like loving a shadow that would never come back. He left her to it and climbed the stairs to the kitchen while the voices on the television yammered on behind him, filling the void caused by their silence.

Brandon opened the door to the kitchen and wasn't surprised to find the room dark. His entire world seemed to have gone dark in the last two months. The basement, his relationship, his mother's house… He thought about opening the drapes and letting some light in but decided against it. He didn't want another fight with his mother, especially not over something as small as letting some sun into her kitchen. The light was always off anymore and he didn't know what she was trying to hide. If it was the condition of the kitchen she was failing spectacularly. He

3

had no problem seeing the spots where the wallpaper was peeling off the walls, or how other sections of the walls were so dirty they appeared black. The low light conditions also did nothing to hide the dirt on the floor.

He didn't know what was going on with her lately. The kitchen looked like it hadn't been cleaned in months. She would have never let the house get like this when he was a kid. Every Sunday morning she had burst into his bedroom with the rising of the sun carrying a bucket of cleaning materials and a smile while ushering him out of bed.

"Sundays are for cleaning and the lord," she'd say as she roused him from his sleep and foisted the bucket upon him. Maryanne Ross liked to be immaculate in house and dress. Who else would already have their hair pulled up, their pearl necklace around their neck, and their apron on at dawn? She looked like June Cleaver had crawled out of an old episode of Leave it to Beaver. He would get out of bed and the next three to four hours were spent cleaning to a steady soundtrack of gospel music and bible sermons coming from the television in the living room at an ear-splitting volume. Maryanne was devout in her Christianity and Pat Robertson's 700 Club was her guiding star.

"IT IS WRITTEN THAT MY FATHER'S HOUSE SHOULD BE A PLACE OF WORSHIP AND YOU'VE TURNED IT INTO A DEN OF THIEVES…" Brandon would do his best to drown it out as he scrubbed until his mother's exaltations rose to match.

"Amen… amen… AMEN!" She would go on until she was screeching and breathless. There were times when his mother's religious fervor scared him. She sounded like a mad woman when she was feeling the spirit and it made the tiny hairs on his body stand up while freezing the deepest recesses of his heart. Sometimes he thought she was mad and truly mad people were capable of anything. Even then he thought her madness had touched him, reached out and hurt him somehow. A fragmented memory of something she did that refused to surface completely.

"Cleanliness is Godliness," she'd remind him when he started to slack off.

"And God is empty just like me June," he'd mutter to himself under his breath as he cleaned the grout between the kitchen floor tiles with a toothbrush.

The same grout that was now stained with dirt.

He stared at the dirty floor with an empty glass in his hand and fought the urge to get the bucket of cleaning supplies and take care of it. He hated those Sundays as a child and yet he now had a Pavlovian need to see it done.

"Is that you Bran-Bran?" His mother's voice came from the living room and he stared daggers at the open doorway where he the light from the television illuminated the darkened walls of the living room in soft, blue light. He hated that name and she knew it.

"Yeah mom. Just getting my medicine,"

He filled his glass with water and turned off the faucet. No matter how hard or far he turned the knob water continued to drip from the end of the faucet stained green from years of hard water. He picked up his pills and dropped them.

"Shit," he tried to trap them against the sink with his hand and succeeded in only knocking them down the drain.

"Damn it," he said and looked at his watch. He had to leave now or risk being late for work.

5

"Did you get your pills?"

"Yeah, all good," he lied and grabbed his lunch from the refrigerator before hurrying out the door.

I should have taken 60. Brandon thought to himself as the traffic on I-376 came to stand still on the hill leading down to the Fort Pitt tunnel. Rain fell from swollen, black clouds and pelted against the windshield. Everything he looked at took on a flat, lifeless, washed-out quality. Was it from the weather, or dropping his pills down the sink? He couldn't be sure. Between dealing with the fallout from the fire, his mother, and Jennifer it was a miracle he remembered to take his medicine at all these days.

He glanced at the clock on the radio and saw it was ten after eight. He took too long getting out of the house and now he was going to be late. The traffic inched along at a snail's pace and again he chastised himself for not taking 60. It was a straight shot and went straight to the road the plant sat on but the unplanned trip down memory lane in the kitchen this morning had knocked him for a loop and wrecked the whole start of his day. He looked around for anything to take his mind off of his current shit show of a life even if only for a couple of minutes and his heart leapt into his throat when he saw the woman in the car next to him.

Looking at her was like looking at a bright light after coming out of a dark room. She looked like Jennifer. Her blonde hair stood out in vivid color against the various shades of gray of everything else. He watched as she kept casting quick glances ahead as she tried to hastily apply eyeliner while they were stopped. She finished with her eyes and turned toward the window. She looked at Brandon and her eyes disappeared into cavernous, sunken sockets. Her jaw slid downward, unhinging like a snake's, turning her mouth into a black, gaping maw as the color drained from her face. Flies flew out of the opening, one or two at first, and progressing until there were what looked like a hundred at a time. The flies flew around her head and landed on the windows, covering them, until she disappeared into a black sea of the wriggling, two winged insects.

Brandon recoiled and looked down at his steering wheel. He balled his hands into fists and rubbed his eyes as hard as he could.

"Not real… not real… not real," he repeated and continued rubbing his eyes until he saw what looked like tiny, light reflecting strips of aluminum foil dancing behind his eyelids. He opened his eyes and chanced a look at her again. He had to be sure. The woman was back to normal, once again putting on makeup, using her visor mirror as a vanity. He placed his trembling hands on his legs and concentrated on the feeling of the fabric as he took a deep breath. His shirt was soaked with sweat and the strong, sulfurous odor of fear filled the car. Brandon found it hard to focus as he continued to stare at her waiting for her to change again.

She looked over but before they could lock eyes, Brandon looked down at his work jacket thrown haphazardly across the passenger seat with the patch on the back that read ALLIED SECURITY. He was having a bad day, but he would be ok once he got to work. He needed some time alone is all. He would talk to Jerry, they were on fairly good terms, and he would ask to be put on perimeter. He would do the hourly walks around the property and the best part would be the solitude. He smiled weakly. He let out a deep breath and began to relax. This would be fine; a little time alone would be exactly what the doctor ordered. Traffic inched forward again and he gave the car some gas. He wanted to put as much distance between him and the woman a car over as possible. Soon he was heading into the tunnel and the further he got beneath Mount Washington the better he felt. As if the mountain and tunnel were a warm, weighted blanket, and he was hidden inside.

—TWO—

"I'll give you the perimeter but I need you to train. I'm sorry," Jerry said, dashing Brandon's hopes not five minutes after he walked through the door. Jerry waddled his overweight frame around his desk and sat down heavily with a sigh. The chair groaned and creaked as Jerry adjusted his sitting position, a grimace on his face.

Brandon stared at the monitors running along the wall while he waited for Jerry to get comfortable. The first screen showed the main gate while the second and third screens showed various parts of the perimeter he wanted to get to so badly.

"Damn sciatica is in rare form today," Jerry said. Brandon was sure a lot of Jerry's back problems came from the fact he was carrying around about three hundred pounds on a small five-foot five frame, but he kept it to himself. Jerry was a good guy as far as bosses went and he was still holding out hope Jerry would change his mind about the training.

"I don't think it's a good idea. Covid protocols remember? Six feet apart and all that," Brandon threw it out there as a hail mary. Jerry stopped shifting around and cocked his eyebrow, a small smile played across his full lips hidden beneath his bushy salt and pepper mustache.

"You're going to be outside. Don't try that bullshit. Besides, did you see her out there? She's a bit of a looker eh? I could ask you to do worse jobs," he said, cocking his eyebrow again.

"I didn't. I'm spoken for remember?"

"Meh," Jerry dismissed him with a wave of his hand. "Everybody has a work wife, no?" He added and Brandon shook his head.

"You're doing it. Let her in. I'm finally comfortable and I'm not moving again," he said, and Brandon knew the subject was closed. He opened the door and for the second time today his heart kicked against his chest as the woman came through the door.

Brandon tried to swallow around the sudden, thick, lump of air in his throat. Vivid color bathed the woman amongst the gray and his mind went back to the woman in the car this morning.

"Brandon, this is Lucinda," he heard Jerry say, and his voice sounded faint, as if it were coming from the other end of a long hallway. In the office light her red hair looked like fire. She looked at him and his breath caught in his throat at the sight of her bright, green eyes. Freckles dusted her cheeks below both eyes and he took a step back as he waited for her full, cherry-colored lips to give way to a black hole in her face. His mind flashed back to the sea of flies in the woman's car and how they covered all the windows like a thick, black blanket. He could feel his heart thudding in his ears. He wiped his sweaty palms against his pants, every muscle in his body wound tight in preparation of the fight or flight response that would come with the flies. Would he run away, or would he swing on this woman he just met? *Are you crazy? You can't hit her in front of your boss. Do you want to lose your job?* He took a slow, steadying breath and forced himself to relax.

"You alright?" Jerry asked.

"Yeah. I told you I'm having a weird day," Brandon said, pulling himself together.

"Alright then. Out of my office both of you. I have things to do," Jerry said.

Gravel crunched and sifted beneath their feet as they walked along the gravel pathway running along the green chain link fence circling the property. Their breath drifted into the wet air and hung there in tiny plumes of vapor as the silence stretched on between them. The morning's rain had slowed to a steady drizzle, but the storm clouds still hovered over them like a dark omen of things to come.

"It's pretty out here," Lucinda said, finally breaking the silence. To their left a small slope made of loose dirt and rocks dropped steeply toward the river. They watched a barge drive by pushing out small waves of dark, grotty water in its wake as it continued down river past the football stadium that sat on the opposite bank. Behind the stadium towering skyscrapers of metal and glass dominated the sky.

"You should be here on a summer night when the fountain is going and all the lights reflect off the water," Brandon said, finally lowering his guard. She looked across the water and found the fountain he was talking about. Today it was off.

"That sounds nice. I'm sorry I messed up your day," she said.

"You didn't. I had a bad morning and was looking forward to being alone. I'm the one who should be sorry.

11

I'm sure that's not how you wanted your first day to start," he said and smiled at her. Her eyes hadn't disappeared and no flies had come frothing out of her mouth yet. Brandon took this as a sign she was safe to be around. *How do you know if that means she's safe, or even if the fly lady was dangerous? You've never seen anything like that before today.* He thought about his mother's religious fervor for the second time today and how he had always thought her mad. Did she pass something on to him? Was he starting to lose it? Seeing fly faced people had to be worse than just being really exuberant in your love for Jesus didn't it? If he was being honest he hadn't been right since the accident when he was eight years old. *Can we not?* His inner voice asked him from the deep recesses of his mind. The day was bad enough without throwing this on top of it. Brandon pushed it down and focused on Lucinda instead.

She smiled at him and it lit up her whole face. It was then Brandon saw what Jerry was talking about. Her uniform was a little big for her and had a baggy look because of it, but outside of that she was quite pretty. Definitely a "looker" as Jerry had so eloquently put it.

"I don't think I've ever met another Lucinda,"

"That was my mother's doing. You can call me Lucy,"

"Lucy," he repeated as if trying it on. " I like it,"

"I'm glad. I was so worried," she said, and rolled her eyes with a smile on her face. They both laughed and walked along as they fell into a more comfortable silence this time. For a while, the only noises were the sounds of the pattering rain and the flowing current of the turgid river.

His thoughts went to Jennifer like they always did during his quiet moments at work. He didn't have to wonder what she was doing while he was gone all day. He knew she was sitting in the recliner, doing nothing but watching television. He hated the thought of her sitting alone in the basement with no one to talk to. She would never go upstairs because she hated his mother. She hated any female he talked to that wasn't her. He would never be able to tell Jennifer about training Lucy today. If he did she would get paranoid and jealous and ride him until he quit his job. Brandon didn't want to quit; he liked his job. He was coming up on having ten years in, way too late to start over somewhere else. He was honestly surprised Jennifer and his mother didn't get along. They were both the same in how they wanted to control every aspect of his life and nothing he did was ever good enough for either one of them.

"So what exactly goes on here?" Lucy asked.

"Hmm?" Brandon asked as he pushed the thoughts of lonely, jealous, Jennifer sitting alone in the basement away.

"The plant. What exactly happens here?" She asked again.

"Defense contract stuff. Motherboards for Predator drones,"

"Are these necessary?" Lucy asked and pointed to the taser and gun holstered on opposites sides of her hips.

"Every once in a while you'll get a drunk person coming up to the gate on a dare as they and their friends bar crawl up and down Carson Street but no, I've never had to shoot or tase anybody,"

"Really? That's disappointing,"

"First time for everything though,"

"A girl can dream," she said. Brandon laughed again and even though the rain was showing no signs of stopping and everything still looked washed out to him, he was glad Jerry had stuck to his guns about him training today. Lucy was alright.

Brandon struggled to open the crooked, wooden, outside basement door without dropping the takeout boxes in his hands and came in to find Jennifer exactly where he knew he would. Sitting in the recliner watching television.

"Hey sweetheart. Did you have a good day?" He asked though he already knew the answer. Jennifer didn't bother to look his way, instead she stayed focused on the television as if he weren't there. Brandon sighed and sat the food down on the rickety table in the corner of the room that served as their kitchen.

"The day started off a little rough but work wasn't too bad," he continued trying to engage her while he opened the boxes of Chinese food. She continued to ignore him and a spark of anger ignited white hot in his mind. A part of him wanted to throw the box of rice at her head. He could almost feel the satisfaction that would come with it thudding against her head. Not because he wanted to hurt her, but because he was tired of being ignored. Brandon took a deep breath, extinguishing his anger and tamped on the embers. He put a set of chopsticks in the box and tried to hand it to her. She turned her nose up at it and went back to the television. The anger tried to come roaring back but he kept it down. While it was true her cold attitude bothered him it wasn't her fault. It was his. She had been fine before the fire and he knew he wouldn't take being

14

covered in burns well if the tables were reversed. He hadn't been there when she needed him the most. He deserved her scorn.

"Come on. You've got to eat," he said gently as possible.

"Do I? What's the point? What's the point in anything when I look like this?" Jennifer asked. He sat the box of rice on the floor next to her recliner and rubbed her arm. He needed her to eat. He couldn't watch her waste away. Over the last couple of months he had gone back and forth on whether he did the right thing pulling her out of the fire or not. She couldn't get past the scars. Maybe it would have been better had he let her die quickly that night instead of the slow death she was engaging in now in this damp basement.

"Why didn't you let me die?" She asked, putting his thoughts into words. Brandon shuddered.

"Because you mean the world to me. You're still my beautiful girl,"

"Liar," she said. He gave up and opened his own box of Beef Lo Mein. The aroma of garlic, soy sauce, and sesame oil made his stomach grumble. He grabbed a wad of noodles with his sticks and found himself thinking about Lucy as he took his first bite. What was she doing right now? Whatever it was it had to be better than this. He looked forward to going to work tomorrow and it was the first time he had looked forward to anything in a while. He turned his attention to the television and took another bite.

"What are we watching?"

"Me, Myself, and Irene," she said.

"Oh, this is a good one," he said and watched Jim Carrey throw himself around on the screen and suddenly

Brandon was a teenager again. Sitting on the enclosed porch at his uncle's house, sweat clinging to his skin while the sounds of crickets and other night insects floated through the screened windows on the sticky summer air while he and his cousins watched In Living Color on a small RCA television. They had always watched tv outside at night because his uncle worked the graveyard shift at the factory and slept through the early evenings. He remembered waking his uncle up once laughing way too loudly at a Fire Marshal Bill sketch.

He settled in with his food and didn't try to get Jennifer to talk again as he focused on the movie. With the way his life had gone over the last couple of months he deserved to unplug and have a laugh or two.

—THREE—

Brandon sat up and rubbed the sleep from his eyes. He had fallen asleep watching the movie but couldn't remember when. He moved the empty Lo Mein box and his mind went blank when he found Jennifer sitting on the bottom edge of the bed. She hadn't left the recliner since they moved into his mother's basement. He smiled at her. Maybe she was starting to come around. Maybe she would start sleeping in bed with him again.

"I'm so glad you're moving around," he said, his voice still thick with sleep. Jennifer turned to face him and the smile fell from his face. The burns on her face were worse. Her skin looked like melted plastic and it slid down her face, looking like a baggy shirt on a skinny frame until it fell from her face, exposing blood, bone, and muscle. He jumped and slid backward as she climbed on the bed on all fours. As she crawled toward him the skin on her arms melted and sloughed off the muscle before hitting the bed with terrible wet sounds. They looked like empty, oversized skin gloves.

"Where are you going lover?" Jennifer cooed. "I thought this is what you wanted. Me back in bed with you. What's wrong? You did this to me. Don't you like it?" He shook his head and moved further back on the bed until he had nowhere left to go. She laughed at him and her voice went from its normal high pitch to a low, guttural growl.

"Come now give us a kiss," she said and lowered her slick, bloody face toward his.

Brandon sat up in bed covered in sweat and stifled the scream aching to come rushing forth from his lungs. He held it in because if he started he wasn't sure he would be able to stop again and having both Jennifer and his mother pissed off at him for waking them up was not the way he wanted to start the day. His mother would want to know what was wrong and regardless of what it was her solution would be more medicine. It had been that way since he was a child, there was nothing more medicine couldn't fix. She spent most of his childhood popping what she had called her mother's little helpers. His medicine was a little more potent than those and he wasn't sure she understood the concept of an overdose… Or she did and was trying to kill him.

He ran his hands through his black, shaggy hair and sighed before scratching at the three days' worth of stubble irritating his jawline. He sat still on the bed as the remnants of the dream refused to leave him. He was convinced the thing that looked like Jennifer was still lurking about, waiting for him somewhere in the darkened basement. Waiting to give him that sloppy, bloody kiss before devouring him in the dark. His heart rattled like machine gun fire in his chest. He slid to the edge of the bed and peered over, convinced he would find it there, half under the bed looking up at him with a smile on its face. Nothing but blood and slime where its skin should have been. It wasn't until he looked over and found Jennifer asleep in the

18

recliner in front of the television like she always was that he allowed himself to relax. He rubbed his eyes again, clearing the last little bit of sleep away and looked at the television. Another movie he hadn't seen in years, Sucker Punch, was on.

He laid back down, his heart still galloping like a runaway horse and didn't need a clock to tell him what time it was. The dull light beginning to come in through the windows let him know it was just before dawn. Brandon closed his eyes. If he fell back to sleep right now he could get two more hours before work. He listened to Jennifer's low, heavy breathing. He hated being up alone in the quiet. The lack of distractions left him alone with his thoughts and there were so many things he didn't want to think about. He didn't want to run through the night of the fire for the millionth time and kick himself for not being home. He didn't want to think about how as a grown man he was back to living in his mother's basement working a job that while not terrible, also wasn't great. Once upon a time he had thought he was destined for something better, but he found out the hard way life didn't care what you thought you were destined for.

Brandon had been a smart kid. School never challenged him. While other kids were learning their numbers and how to add in kindergarten he could already do his multiplication tables up to twelve. It didn't matter what was being taught, he soaked it up like a sponge. All that changed when he was eight and his father died. Then the accident happened.

He remembered almost none of it other than he had hit his head and there was water. Sometimes he would get quick flashes of a memory like he was on the cusp of remembering what happened. He never got there. The memory would always dance in the darker recesses of his brain just out of reach. The same way a word hangs on one's tongue. Right there but at the same time annoyingly out of reach. After the accident he had gone to live with his aunt and uncle for a bit while his mother worked on herself. It was hard for a single parent to raise a boy as challenging as him his uncle had told him.

After he hit his head the world had a tendency to become washed out and faded sometimes. He would lose chunks of time and didn't retain information the same way he used to. The medicine helped with the perception and loss of time issues but there was nothing to be done about the way his brain worked in relation to learning new information. He was by no means stupid, but it took him a little longer to grasp new things.

Melancholy washed over him and chilled him to the bone. He shivered and slid back beneath the heavy comforter on the bed. Adding his responsibility for what happened to Jennifer was a little too much. Was this his life now? Would it always be this way? Getting up every day to work a menial job to make ends meet while both the women in his life nagged him regardless of what he tried to do for them. Would he work himself into an early grave trying to make them happy? Brandon wore his life like a pair of concrete boots, and they might as well have been pulling him to the bottom of the cold, dirty river he walked along every day.

His pulse quickened as the icy water enveloped his mind. The weight pulled him down and he thrashed his arms desperately trying to stay above water. He saw the green chain link fence getting farther away as his arms got tired and he started to sink. His head disappeared beneath the surface and his vision got darker as the less and less rays from the sun were able to penetrate the murky water. A hand broke through the water and reached for him. He grabbed it and held on for dear life as it pulled him up.

Brandon broke the surface of the water choking and gasping for air. He wiped the water from his eyes and saw his savior staring down at him with her perfect red hair and green eyes. Lucy.

He climbed out of bed and headed upstairs; sleep was over for him. He needed to find something productive to do or he would drive himself mad before the sun came up. *There's that word again. Mad.* Brandon thought to himself as he tip toed up the creaking stairs towards the dirty kitchen waiting beyond the basement door.

Brandon stopped scrubbing and wiped the sweat from his brow while he admired his work. The kitchen floor was looking great if he did say so himself. He dropped the toothbrush and massaged his red, trembling hand. He rubbed his fingers and winced when he hit his fingertips. The edges under his nails screamed, they were sensitive from being repeatedly stuck into the bucket of hot water. He looked at his watch, it was a little after seven. He had successfully wiled away the quiet early hours of the morning and could start getting ready for work. He picked up the toothbrush and dropped it into the bucket of dirty water before dumping it all in the sink. Guilt gnawed at him for thinking about Lucy the way he did this morning with Jennifer only sleeping a couple of feet away in the recliner. While it was true all they did was fight anymore and they hadn't laid together since before the fire it was no excuse.

21

He couldn't fault her for acting the way she was. He also didn't want to continue sobbing at the state of his life so he had done what his mother had engrained in him since a young age. He cleaned it all away. He put the bucket back under the sink and took out his medicine. He turned on the faucet and let the water run to clean out the dirt residue from the bucket before getting his glass.

"Are you getting a drink or filling a bathtub out there? Remember, want not waste not Bran-Bran," his mother called out to him from the living room. The word bathtub triggered one of his fragmented memories. He heard a thud and felt a sharp pain in the back of his head. He looked up through watery vision and heard someone's muffled voice but couldn't make out what they were saying. Suddenly, as quick as the memory had come it was gone and Brandon was back in the kitchen gasping for air while the water continued to run.

"Bran-Bran the water," his mother said again. He looked down at the pills lying in his open palm and suppressed the urge to stride into the living room, yank her frail body off the bed, and bash her face in. He slammed the pills down on the counter.

"Stop calling me Bran-Bran God damn it!" He yelled.

"Don't take that tone with me young man, and don't you dare blaspheme the lord's name in my house," her voice broke. "Why are you so mean to your mother? Do you want me dead, is that it? Are you trying to kill me?" She cried from the living room.

"No ma. I just don't like that name is all. I didn't mean to upset you," he said in a softer tone.

"No you did. You hate me," she said.

22

"I don't hate you mom. I didn't sleep well. I'm sorry," he said, and got only sobs from the darkened living room in response. *Now I can add terrible son to terrible boyfriend.* He lamented as he fetched his lunch from the refrigerator and went back downstairs to get ready for work.

He crept down the stairs trying not to wake Jennifer up and found her already awake watching television when he reached the bottom. She looked haggard in the harsh light of the television. The combination of not eating, barely sleeping, and the burns were catching up with her. There was something different about her this morning though. A glint in her eye that had been missing these last couple of months.

"Sorry if I woke you," he said, prepared to get a second tongue lashing in only a matter of minutes but it didn't come.

"It's ok. I've been thinking. You're always asking what you can do to help me and I think I figured it out," Jennifer said.

"Alright what can I do. I'll do anything," he said smiling. The last remnants of his nightmare melted away as he sat down on the bed next to her chair. Finally they could move forward and things could get back to some semblance of how they used to be.

"I want new skin," she said.

"Okay. They can do wonderful things with skin grafts these days. I'll have to pick up a lot of extra shifts, but we can do it. I'll give the doctor a call today during my lunch break-," he stopped talking when she shook her head no.

"That will take too long. You have to get it," she said. He stared at her, a blank look on his face. Was there something he was missing? Was his brain's slow way of processing things rearing its ugly head again.

"I don't understand," Brandon said.

—FOUR—

Brandon sat at the table in the breakroom lost in a daze. People came and went, conversations buzzed around him in loud murmurs but he saw no one and heard nothing. No matter how many times he tried to turn over and tear apart the discussion he and Jennifer had before he left for work this morning he couldn't make sense of it.

She didn't want to go through doctors. When doctors do a skin graft they take skin from another part of the body and move it. She had no unburned skin to move, and even if she did the process of taking skin from one section and grafting it to another would be painful. Did he want her to go through more pain? She had asked.

"Then what is it you want me to do?" He asked.

"Do you remember Silence of the Lambs?"

Did he remember Silence of the Lambs? How could he not? No one could forget Buffalo Bill dancing around his basement to Goodbye Horses with his penis tucked back between his legs while asking if someone would fuck him. Is that what Jennifer wanted? Crying women held hostage in the basement and lotion in baskets?

"Earth to Brandon are you there?"

Brandon snapped back to the break room to find Lucy standing there looking at him as if he had grown an extra head. His mind lingered on Jennifer a moment longer. He had to have misunderstood. There was no way Jennifer expected him to make her a skin suit. Even if she did, how did she think that was going to happen? He didn't want to kill anyone and it wasn't like he could take a stroll downtown to Skins R' Us and ask the pleasant man standing behind the counter if he could give him something in a size five foot three with blonde hair and a pale complexion.

"Brandon?" Lucy asked again and waved her hand in front of his face.

"Yeah? Sorry," he said, happy for the distraction. He didn't want to think about skin or how to get it anymore.

"Everything alright?" She asked him. He watched as she pulled up a chair and sat down at the other side of the table.

The tiny lunchroom had four tables, all of them full while the people who had nowhere to sit stood around talking. Brandon never did understand why they would have everyone go to lunch at the same time when there weren't enough tables for everyone. He hated the tiny lunchroom because it reminded him of his tiny basement. It felt like the only time he got to stretch his legs or stand to his full height anymore was when he was walking the perimeter around the plant. His entire life was like a tiny box and the walls were closing in on him inch by inch, day by day until soon they would drive the breath from his lungs and leave him nothing more than a desiccated husk crushed below the heavy wheel of time and responsibilities.

He watched Lucy as she unwrapped a Twinkie and took it down half of it in one bite.

"What?" She asked, her cheeks puffed out like a chipmunk's storing nuts. She smiled around the cream and half chewed, yellow spongy cake in her mouth.

"I like to eat," she said and, he was struck by the sudden crazy desire to ask her if she'd like to go get something to eat after work sometime but he quashed it. He remembered how she had looked after she pulled him out of the water in his mind this morning. She had looked like an angel. He took out his own lunch, a turkey sandwich with cheese and tomato on wheat bread and a bottle of cherry limeade sparkling water.

"Now see, this is a lunch," he said as Lucy produced a second Twinkie from her lunch bag and unwrapped it.

"Listen. Do you see the way this uniform hangs on me? I need to fatten up a little bit. So you go ahead and stick to your turkey sandwich Mr. Tight Shirt," she said.

"Are you calling me fat?" Brandon asked, feigning outrage. Lucy looked at him and scrunched her face as she gave him a once over.

"You have more of a dad bod going on," she said.

"That's a subtle way of saying I'm fat,"

"Nah you're just a little thicc. Momma likes it," she said, and winked at him as she took another bite of her Twinkie. He smirked and started in on his sandwich. Where had the shy girl who had stared at the floor in Jerry's office on her first day gone? Also, why did her liking his body type make him feel warm inside? He was getting close to a line he shouldn't cross and yet he wanted to anyway.

"It's so much nicer out here when it isn't cold and rainy," Lucy said as they did their daily walk around the perimeter. A slight breeze blew in off the river bringing a vinegary smell with it.

"Ugh, what is that smell?" She asked and covered her nose with her shirt.

"That would be the Ohio River," Brandon said.

"Why does it smell like this today?"

"Because it's the most polluted river in the United States and on certain days when the wind is just right you get treated to the gift of its acrid aroma. Still, in the summer I take my lunches out here and watch the boats go up and down the river," he said and watched the current go by in lazy, even rushes.

"Aw we should totally do that sometime," she said. He didn't know if she was being serious or not but it sounded like she was. He had never been able to tell when a woman was into him. Unless they wore a flashing neon sign that said: HEY I'M INTO YOU. He had nothing. Reading signals wasn't his forte. He didn't know if it was another byproduct of the head injury or not. He hadn't had much practice with flirting girls at eight years old. She looked at him and smiled. The sunlight caught her hair and it looked like a blanket of flowing copper.

"Do you live close to the city?" He asked, once again trying not to broach the subject of asking her out.

"No. I'm about a half an hour away. I live in a tiny town called Canonsburg. Are you familiar with it?" She asked.

"Yes I know where Canonsburg is. When I was little I lived with my aunt and uncle in McDonald for a while. They share a border," he said.

"How about you? Do you live across the river somewhere in there?" Lucy asked and pointed at the tall buildings towering across the river.

"No. I live in Crafton," he said.

"Anything interesting there?"

"Not at all. It's nothing but businesses, motels, and restaurants with a state route running through the middle of it," he said.

They walked on and every so often the sun would catch her face and highlight the random spattering of freckles dancing across the tops of her cheeks below her eyes. They looked like a smattering of tiny islands in the radiant and smooth unending sea of peach that was her skin. The thought of her skin brought him back to Jennifer and her request. It was still a dark rabbit hole he didn't want to go down where each question had answers more horrible than the last. Where would he get the skin? No one would give up their skin willingly and so he would have to take it. How would he attach it? He would have to sew it together. He didn't know how to sew and the thought of sewing strips of human skin together created a mash up in his head equal parts Sally from The Nightmare Before Christmas and Leatherface. Then there was treating the skin, he knew hunters tanned skins to make animal blankets. Would this be the same kind of situation and lastly, he wouldn't be able to let someone go after he took pieces of their skin. That was a safe way to end up in jail real fast. He didn't know if he had it in him to kill anybody. Still, her being stuck in the fire was his fault and he had told her he'd do anything.

"Hey are you alright?" Lucy asked and gave his shoulder a shake.

"Yeah. I'm sorry,"

"You keep going away today. Where do you go?"

"You wouldn't believe me if I told you,"

"We should hang out after work sometime and get a drink. I've never been into the city," she said, letting the subject drop.

"Sure," he said before he could stop himself. What was he doing? Nothing. Friends could have drinks Brandon convinced himself. It didn't have to mean anything romantic. He knew Jennifer would disagree but it would be fine as long as she never found out. He deserved a life outside of her and work, and the thought of spending time with someone who didn't want anything from him or wasn't going to spend the whole time belittling him sounded nice.

"When were you thinking?" He asked.

Brandon pulled his little gray four door with the rusty bumper into the driveway and sat in the car for a few minutes after he turned it off. He took time to savor the last few minutes of silence he was going to have today. On most days he would have given anything for Jennifer to engage with him, to acknowledge he was there, but now he didn't want to talk because Jennifer could be like a dog with a bone and he knew the second he walked into the house she would want to talk about the skin.

He stared through the windshield and contemplated not going inside at all. He considered starting the car and backing out of the driveway before anyone knew he was home. Where would he go? What would he do? Didn't matter. He could grab Lucy and just drive. No more mother, no more Jennifer. No more crazy talk about skin.

His life could be better. It could be more than this. Brandon's hand hovered over the key and he almost turned it in the ignition before reality came crashing back down on him. *"You're a pathetic excuse for a man,"* Jennifer's voice hurled one of her favorite insults in his head. He took the key out of the ignition and hung his head. She was right. It was his fault and for months he'd been looking for anything to make her better, and now, when she had given him a way he wanted to turn tail and run.

"Fuck… fuck… fuck," Brandon said and punctuated each one with a headbutt against the steering wheel. He looked up to find the neighbor from the house behind theirs staring at him. He gave her a weak smile and a wave.

"Do you really think you are capable of killing someone?" He asked himself, daring to acknowledge the thought out loud for the first time. Brandon watched the woman drop her trash in the can on her back porch. *Could you kill her?* He tried to picture himself doing it.

He would get out of the car and yell for her to wait while he crossed their conjoined backyards. He could make up a reason for wanting to talk to her like asking her if she's ever had any issues with people messing with her car. He was only asking because more than once he had come out to go to work in the morning to find new scratches on his that weren't there the day before. He would strike while she was thinking about it, her guard down. How would he strike was the next question? He was a bigger guy. *"You're a little thick,"* he heard Lucy's voice. Could he knock the woman out with one, solid punch? Brandon didn't know. He could spin her around and wrap one of his meaty forearms around her neck and pull up with his arm while

31

pushing down on her head and choke her out. She would fight but it would only be a matter of time before she succumbed due to the lack of blood flow to the brain, but how long would that take? Every minute he fought with her would be more time for someone else to come out of their house or for someone to pass by and see them.

The woman waved back and Brandon was back in the driver's seat of his car. He watched her go in the house and took a breath. His stomach was in knots and churned as if it were filled with a thousand angry bees. Bees that were also on fire. He choked back the bile rising in his throat and closed his eyes. This wasn't going to work. If he couldn't think about killing somebody without getting sick to his stomach how was he supposed to actually accomplish the deed? He couldn't. Jennifer was just going to have to deal with it.

The sanctuary of the dark kitchen greeted him like a familiar friend and calmed him. He sat down at the kitchen table, closed his eyes, and massaged his temples. After a couple minutes he opened them again and readied himself to go to the basement when he saw the familiar glow of the television painting the doorway in low, blue light from the living room.

Brandon got up and walked close enough to the doorway where he could see the television but not close enough to let his mother know he was there. On the television a preacher was gesticulating wildly, a thick bible held up in his right hand. He brandished the book like a weapon against the sinners and the other undesirables.

"WHAT COMES OUT OF A PERSON IS WHAT DEFILES THEM!" He screamed and continued as the members of his congregation clapped and shouted amen.

"FOR IT IS FROM WITHIN, OUT OF A PERSON'S HEART, THAT EVIL THOUGHTS COME — SEXUAL IMMORALITY, THEFT, MURDER, ADULTERY, GREED, MALICE, DECEIT, LEWDNESS, ENVY, SLANDER, ARROGANCE, AND FOLLY. ALL THESE EVILS COME FROM INSIDE AND DEFILE A PERSON!" Spittle flew from pursed lips of the preacher's red face as he screamed the name of every sin. Brandon came into the living room now to find his mother staring at the television transfixed, completely in the grip of the spirit. She wasn't in her tiny, dark, living room. She was riding the religious lightning white hot, a terrible smile etched into her face and again he thought of madness.

"Have you decided?" Jennifer asked him not two seconds after his feet hit the basement floor. Brandon plopped down on the bed and put his hands over his face. He still heard the preacher's ranting about murder and defilement echoing in his mind. Jennifer wanted him to defile himself. While he never liked the religious stuff he never had decided whether he believed in it or not. However, if it was true, then killing for skin would damn him to an eternity in hell burning in the lake of fire. His brain seized on the image of him burning. *Isn't that what I left Jennifer to do? Didn't I let her burn?* He thought to himself. She had burned, was he too good to burn?

Brandon opened his eyes and looked at her expectant face through his splayed fingers. Her face held a mixture of eagerness and excitement, she looked like a child on Christmas morning. He didn't want to disappoint her but he was also sure he wouldn't be able to kill anyone. Maybe he could talk her out of it, convince her to see reason and see a legitimate doctor.

"Are you sure this is what you want?" He asked her and watched the smile fade from her face.

"I should have known you wouldn't have the stomach for it. So much for you being willing to do anything for me," she said, and turned away from him.

"I'm just saying I think a doctor is the way to go for this one. I don't think I can kill anybody and what if I mess up and you get an infection?" He asked. He thought the point about an infection was solid and would make her see reason. He should have known better. She stared him down with a withering look that could peel paint from a wall.

"Well Bran-Bran," she said using his mother's favorite pet name fully aware of how much he hated it.

"What is it you can do? You didn't stop me from burning and now you can't fix me either. You're pathetic," she finished and his blood boiled.

Brandon leapt from the bed, red circles forming on the edges of his vision. He couldn't take her ungrateful, incessant nagging anymore. It was like he was outside his body as he watched her eyes go wide when he wrapped his hands around her throat and pushed her backward. The recliner toppled over sending them both spilling to the cold, concrete floor. He straddled her and tightened his grip around her throat.

"If you're so unhappy I'll finish the job the fire started you bitch," he said.

She wriggled beneath him and clawed at his arms as she struggled to breathe. *Come on just a little longer and you'll be free.* He thought to himself as tears ran from her eyes. She stopped clawing and her body started to go limp when Brandon came to his senses and let go.

Jennifer took a deep breath and went into a coughing fit. He climbed off of her, a deep feeling of revulsion settling into every fiber of his being. What had he almost done? Like she didn't have it hard enough already. He, as the one person who was supposed to protect her had now let a fire almost kill her and then almost killed her himself.

"I see how it is," she said regaining her breath. "You can kill me but you can't kill for me," she said. Brandon recoiled as if he had been smacked in the face. She was right. He was pathetic. He had to fix it.

"Okay. I'll do what you want. I'll get you your skin," he said, resigned to his fate.

—FIVE—

Sunlight reflected off the pages of Brandon's book making it hard to read. He squinted his eyes while he reread the paragraph about sewing with a running stitch. His practice stitches had been huge and clumsy at first, but over the last couple weeks he felt he was starting to tighten them up. Things had returned to some version of what he considered normal in the days since he had tried to strangle Jennifer on the basement floor.

Even now he could still see the look of wild terror in her eyes. The absolute certainty she was about to die etched into every line of her face. Part of him enjoyed it. He had never lashed out like that before and it equal parts scared and excited him. He still wasn't looking forward to killing anyone, but he now knew he could do it.

He finished off the last bite of his apple and dropped the used-up core into the crumpled brown bag sitting next to him and stared across the water at the downtown Pittsburgh skyline from where he sat on the slope of the bank leading to the river. He was going to kill someone in there tonight. The thought of it made him queasy but it had to be done, Jennifer was growing impatient. During one of her more insolent episodes he had let her know they were doing it on his timetable or not at all. He had to prepare. If he got caught who would get her skin? Who would take care of her then? She thought it over and accepted his terms but her patience was wearing thin. Brandon knew he couldn't put her off anymore.

In the intervening time he had researched the best way to incapacitate someone. He wanted something quick and quiet and found his original idea of choking someone out was his best bet. A little extra pressure on the windpipe with his forearm and they would be unable to scream.

"I was wondering where you disappeared to," Lucy said as she came trudging down the gravel pathway toward where he was sitting.

"I told you I take my lunches out here sometimes," he said, and closed the book before tucking it away under his leg.

"In the summertime you said. We're on the tail end of spring here," she said, and sat down next to him. She leaned close and a sweet fragrance of vanilla filled his nose. Warm shockwaves of electricity shot through his body.

"What are you reading there?" She asked. Her warm breath lingered on his cheek and his heart skipped a beat. Again he found himself wanting to run away with her and leave this lunacy behind. Instantly his conscience kicked in and made him feel like garbage. How could he think of doing that to Jennifer? He had to take care of her. He had to fix what he had allowed to happen to her. He took the book out from under his leg and showed it to Lucy sheepishly. She took it and flipped it over.

"Sewing for Beginners," she read the titled and arched her eyebrow. Her lips hinted at a playful smirk.

"What? You'd be amazed how many of these things I rip," he lied and looked down at his pants.

"We should get that drink I was talking about tonight. What do you say?" Lucy asked. He looked at her open, smiling face and a sudden urge to kiss her roared to life and begged to be let out. Brandon forced it back into an empty room in his mind and boarded the door shut before he could do something so stupid as act on the impulse. *Why shouldn't I?* He thought to himself. The two women in his life demanded so much of him. Two women who had no regard for his wants or needs in any way. He wished he was as strong as his big frame suggested. Strong enough to tell them both to go to hell. Instead he was lonely, and this beautiful woman, for whatever reason wanted to spend time with him and didn't want him to murder anyone in return for it.

"I can't tonight. How about Friday?" Brandon asked, giving in.

"It's a date," she said, and joined him in staring across the water. They spent the rest of their lunchbreak sitting there in silence, feeling no need to break it, instead being content just being in each other's presence.

Brandon scanned the club and stayed close to the bar. Pink and blue neon lights ran along the walls covering the club in a pink and blue glow. Loud music with thunderous bass pounded from the speakers at a volume that rattled his ear drums.

He watched the people grinding their bodies against each other on the dance floor and had no desire to join them. He had absolutely no rhythm and he didn't want to draw attention to himself. He was sure people would remember a stocky white man flailing about on the dance floor like he was having a seizure. The whole scene was chaos and Brandon wished he was anywhere but here. He should have taken Lucy up on her offer. *Focus. Jennifer is waiting for you. You don't want to let her down.* A woman came up to the bar and ordered a drink. He watched her out of the corner of his eye and went over his preparations.

He had stopped home after work to change and get what he needed for tonight. Mostly what he needed was courage. Brandon had never been a violent man by nature. Even as a boy he had been content to let the other kids in his grade bully him even though he was already two times bigger than all of them. His uncle had always referred to him as a gentle giant. He remembered sitting in their sunbathed kitchen one spring day while his uncle tried to explain to him the concept of righteous anger. He understood what it was but he still internalized while seeking to avoid confrontation. His attack on Jennifer was the first time he had ever lashed out at anybody.

The only thing he ended up taking with him were the heavy duty, plastic zip ties he used for work. He threw the zip ties in his trunk along with his work jacket and identification. He figured the three items looked better together if he were to get stopped by the police for some reason than if he only had the ties.

"Do you have a preference?" He had asked Jennifer before leaving. The whole thing was macabre and insane, but since the skin was going on her he thought he should take what she did or didn't want into account.

"I've always wanted a tattoo," she said, and manipulated her mouth into a grotesque attempt of a smile. A nice smile was hard to pull off when most of your lips were missing and what was left was burned and twisted scar tissue.

"You need a refill my man?" The bartender asked him and Brandon was back in the pulsating nightclub. He looked down at his glass and nodded while handing it over.

"Still just Coke?"

"Yes. Thank you," Brandon said, and looked at the woman again. With her shoulder length brown hair and short stature she reminded him of a younger version of his mother. She took a drink and shimmied her shoulders in time with the music. She took another sip and closed her eyes while she swayed. Whoever this woman was she was feeling the music and it was infectious. It made him want to dance too. The bartender returned with his drink and Brandon reached for it at the same time the woman turned to leave the bar. They bumped into each other and she dropped her glass, sending her drink spilling all over the bar. She let out an exasperated sigh as they both reached for her tipped over glass. His breath caught in his throat, there was a tattoo on her wrist.

The tattoo consisted of a group of different sized, offset stars with a smattering of small, multicolored dots made to look like a galaxy in between them.

"Sorry," Brandon said, and reached for a stack of napkins while the woman picked up the now empty glass. The woman looked up at him and her eyes disappeared down deep, black, sockets. Her mouth unhinged and Brandon jumped back. He hurriedly left the bar and disappeared into the sea of people on the dance before the flies could come.

He hid among the dancers until his heartbeat slowed down and his hands stopped trembling. He moved through the crowd and took up residence against the opposite wall. A not small part of him wanted to flee the club without looking back but he couldn't. There would be accusations and a fight if he came home without a body, and if he didn't do it tonight he didn't know if he'd ever be able to get up the nerve again.

Brandon watched the woman from across the dance floor for the rest of the night. She couldn't be human could she? Neither her nor the woman from the car. Human's eyes didn't disappear and their jaws didn't become open caverns spitting out flies. The question now was what were they? Not that it mattered, the bigger implication to Brandon was he could kill them without feeling guilty. In fact, he'd be doing the world a favor wouldn't he? His headache cleared up and the queasiness he'd been feeling since lunch melted away. This was fine. This he could do.

He spent the rest of the night hanging out on the far wall with occasional trips to the bar to refill his coke. He wasn't big on alcohol. It made his head fuzzy and since he already didn't operate at optimal thinking capacity due to his accident he didn't need anything to make it worse. Brandon watched the woman (was he even sure she was one?) drink and dance. At first he watched to see if she was alone, and once he knew she was it became about not letting her out of his sight. He didn't want to miss her leave.

A couple hours later, he wasn't sure as he had long since lost track of time, he watched her finish her last drink and pay the tab. He downed the last of his and sat the glass down on an empty table as he passed by. Brandon headed for the door keeping his pace deliberate. He wanted her to exit first.

The cool night air stung his face. It felt a lot colder than it was after leaving the hot and humid confines of the club. He looked around and found the street was empty except for the two of them. A cooler than usual summer night to keep the street empty of witnesses. It was like God knew what she was and wanted him to succeed. *Enough with the God shit.* Brandon thought to himself and again he saw his mother saying amen over and over, rising in volume until she was no longer saying it, but instead, crying it out in rapturous ecstasy. It wasn't a road he wanted to go down. *"What comes out of a person defiles them,"* the preacher's voice echoed in his head. He remembered the preacher had listed murder as a defilement. What did it mean when literal flies poured out of someone's mouth? What kind of defilement was that?

He fell in behind the woman and kept pace. It wasn't hard to do. She didn't so much walk as she staggered down the sidewalk. He let this continue until she got to the front of the alley where he had parked his car. *What are the chances?* Brandon thought. She had three ways she could have gone after leaving the club and she just happened to pick the one that lead straight toward where he had parked. Some might call that providence. *"Others might call what you're doing apophenia,"* his inner voice shot back.

"Excuse me," Brandon called out and ran to catch up. He prepared himself for what he was going to see when she turned around and yet the lack of eyes and empty sockets still knocked him back.

"I'm not from here. Could you tell me where Penn Avenue is?" He asked, pushing on through his terror at her features. Before she could say anything he grabbed her and pulled her into the alley. He wrapped his forearm around her throat from behind and applied the pressure the way the video had said. It didn't take her long to pass out. He drug her behind his car and zip tied her wrists and ankles before depositing her in the trunk. He spared one last look around and when he was satisfied he hadn't been seen he climbed in the car.

A minute later he pulled out of the alley and took the first bridge across the river. He drove along the empty streets of the neighborhood everyone knew as the North Shore. Brandon looked out the window and he could see the plant he worked at lit up in the dark. He saw no one walking the perimeter and thought about Lucy. He saw her red hair and freckles, and her pretty smile. He suddenly felt melancholic. He wished he was at work with her right now taking one of their walks.

Brandon drove on across another bridge. It's large, yellow metal girders looked orange in the glow of the streetlights. His was the only car passing over at this late hour. At the other end he drove under the train trestle. It's black, iron frame being held up by a thick wall of cracked bricks and mortar. It was a straight shot home now. He picked up speed while still making sure to stay within the legal limit. He didn't want to get pulled over now. He tried to stop his thoughts from going back to Lucy again as the city shrank behind him.

Thirty minutes later Brandon pulled into his driveway and turned off the car to hear the muffled screams of the woman coming from the trunk. He looked around the neighborhood and nothing but quiet streets and darkened houses greeted him.

"You idiot," he said. He had been so focused on the zip ties to keep someone restrained he never gave thought to them waking up and needing to keep them quiet. Brandon exited the car and ran in the house. A few moments later he returned with a roll of duct tape. He ripped off a moderately sized strip and knelt next to the trunk.

"I'm going to open the trunk. If you scream I'll kill you do you understand?" He asked, keeping his voice low as to not attract attention. Brandon didn't know who in the neighborhood might be night owls. He was going to kill her anyway but she didn't need to know that until it was too late for her to do anything about it.

"Yes," her muffled voice replied from inside the trunk. He lifted the door and as soon as it was open she tried to scream. He had anticipated that and it was why he had a strip ripped and waiting. He slapped the tape across her mouth and shot a glance around the neighborhood again. He stood stone still in the dark watching and waiting for a light to turn on, or for someone to stick their head out of their front door. When none of these things happened he pulled her out of the trunk, threw her over his shoulder and carried her into the house. She wouldn't leave alive.

"What did you bring me?" Jennifer asked almost giddy when he brought the woman in and laid her down on their small kitchen table. He tried to ignore the fact Jennifer had asked *what* he had brought her and not *who*. The woman struggled against the zip ties and looked around the basement with her empty sockets. The thought she might still be able to see even without eyes gave Brandon a chill.

"Does she have a tattoo? Let me get a look at her," Jennifer said pushing past him. He let her by and pointed out the tattoo on her wrist.

"Ooooh I like it," she said, and clapped. Her childhood exuberance didn't last long.

"I like the tattoo but not much else. I mean look, she has freckles," Jennifer said in a disgusted tone. Brandon saw Lucy and her perfect freckles and Jennifer's remark offended him to the core of his being.

"We can maybe use this body for a couple of pieces but you're going to have to get another one," Jennifer went on.

"Why are you never happy?" He asked and in that moment he realized he'd been essentially dating his mother. She was never happy either and she had picked at him his whole life until he did everything she wanted exactly how she wanted it. He hated it. He had always hated it. How did he let this happen?

Brandon looked down at the woman on the table and didn't want to do this anymore, but he had no other options. He couldn't let her go. He was already looking at a kidnapping charge just for what he'd done so far.

"I'll be happy when you finally do something right," Jennifer said and he wanted backhand her, or wrap his hands around her throat again. Anything to make her stop talking.

He reached down and wrapped his hands around the woman's throat instead. He couldn't let her go. It had to be this way. He no longer saw a woman with no eyes. Instead he saw Jennifer, the way she had been the other night. Brandon squeezed harder until he was red in the face and spittle hung from his bottom lip. He watched her struggle and kick against the table which groaned and shimmied beneath her, threatening to break as the legs bucked and slid against the concrete floor. Soon her movements slowed but he wouldn't stop early again. He kept on the pressure until she moved no more. A sense of profound relief flooded him as he thought about how he'd never have to hear her nag him again. Until he looked over and saw the real Jennifer watching with a rapturous smile on her face.

Brandon removed his hands from the woman's throat, his hands trembling from exertion, sweat clinging to his skin. Shame washed over him in a black tidal wave and threatened to drown him. Jennifer put something in his hand and he looked down to see himself holding a knife.

"You've come this far. You can go the rest of the way," she said. Jennifer wanted a tattoo and that's where he started. With a shaking hand, he slid the knife into the dead woman's wrist and began to cut.

—SIX—

Brandon looked up at Jennifer every couple of seconds as he sewed the tattoo covered flap of skin to her wrist. What he saw made him nervous. She watched him with a huge smile on her face. He had expected her to jump or flinch with every stitch yet she sat stone still. It was he who was experiencing a deep unsettling feeling in his stomach that brought him to the edge of vomiting while she was completely unfazed. She watched him with the same curiosity and detachment one would devote to a science experiment.

He finished and sterilized the area before he wrapped it in gauze. Her getting an infection was the last thing he needed. He didn't want to deal with the complaining that would come with it. She would never see it as an accident. She would be convinced he did it on purpose to make her suffer and then she would engage in her favorite past time of telling him he couldn't do anything right.

"Alright. It's done," he said, and looked up at her again. An intense wave of hatred washed over him red and hot. Brandon stood up from the small wooden chair and went back to the body. He wanted nothing more than to tell Jennifer to get out but he knew she had nowhere to go. No friends, no family, only him. He couldn't do it. No matter how much he wanted to. He was firmly trapped. The cement boot that was their relationship suddenly felt heavier than it ever had before. The basement felt smaller as if the walls were closing in on him and he struggled to breathe. He needed a way out and strongly considered the next person he should kill would be himself.

He stared down at the body now lying face down on the table with two strips of skin removed from its back. Both excisions were medium-sized, triangle shaped flaps removed from over her scapulae. Even in the basement's dim lighting her exposed blood coated muscles glistened as if they were smeared with KY Jelly. Brandon grimaced and removed the flaps of skin from the clothesline he had strung above the table. He checked the skin, his stomach tying itself knots.

"I think they are ready. Do you want to do them now or wait?" He asked. He hoped she would opt for now, he wanted to get all of this over with.

"I've been waiting for months. Let's do it now,"

"Alright," he threaded the needle and helped Jennifer take off her shirt. For the first time, he almost wished he drank. He could have used something to take the edge off and steady his hands. Brandon laid the piece of skin on her burned back and sewed it in place with a running stitch while he summoned every ounce of will power he had not to lose his dinner all over the floor. He already had enough of a mess to clean up. He didn't want to add to it.

Brandon sat at the small table tucked back into the corner of the break room. His countenance took on a pale, waxy appearance under the bright fluorescent lights. The dark bags under his eyes stood out in stark contrast to the paleness of the rest of his face. He took a bite of his sandwich and his head dropped.

The moment his eyes closed Brandon was back in his basement of horrors. Back amongst his carnage of blood and skin. He saw the dead woman, he hadn't even bothered to learn her name, lying face down on the table, her arm dangling off the side. Her limp hand rested against the cold, concrete floor. The metallic odor of her blood hung in the air.

His eyes snapped open as quickly as they had shut. He was back in the too brightly lit break room. He dropped his sandwich on the table, his appetite gone. *It's better you didn't know her name.* He told himself. It was like when you took in a stray you didn't intend to keep. It was all over if you gave it a name. Names created feelings, connections, a bond between them.

"Don't take this the wrong way but you look like shit," Lucy said and sat down. He tried to give her a smile but he didn't have the energy.

"Are you okay? Are you sick?" she asked. She slid her chair closer to his and put her hand against his head. He saw the concern on her face and he couldn't remember the last time Jennifer had shown concern for him.

"I didn't get much sleep,"

"Rough night?" She asked. She didn't know the half of it and he could never tell her. After he finished working on Jennifer, he spent the rest of the night scrubbing the blood off the floor. Most of it came clean but the mortar used to fill the previous cracks in the floor caused by water damage were stained red. They would never be gray again. He put anything bloody in a garbage bag. The worst part, the part that kept him up long after the cleaning was done happened when he rolled the woman's body back over. She no longer had black empty sockets where her eyes should have been. Instead, he found two icy blue eyes staring back at him, and for the rest of the night her empty eyes watched him everywhere he went.

Now that she had what she wanted from him, Jennifer had returned to normal behavior of pretending he didn't exist. She fell asleep in front of the television and snored away while he continued to clean. At four am he finished and finally slept. The dead woman's icy blue eyes followed him into his dreams.

"Nightmares. I've had night terrors since I was a kid," Brandon said, and it wasn't a lie. He knew he could never tell her the truth but he didn't feel right lying to her either. Half-truths would have to suffice.

"I have a recurring night terror where I'll be lying in bed and I'll be convinced an evil entity is in the room with me. I call him the shadow man because he looks like a black, featureless shape. He sits on my chest and it feels like I can't breathe. I try to scream or move but nothing comes out and I'm stuck in place like I'm a prisoner in my own body," Brandon said, and suddenly he wondered if that was how the woman had felt last night while she was zip tied on the table unable to move or fight back while he took her breath away.

"I understand. I have nightmares myself. Although nothing as pants-shittingly terrifying as what you just described," Lucy said, and put her hand over his. His heart sped up and his insides felt like they were on fire but he made no attempt to move his hand.

"What are yours about?" He asked.

"Mainly my mother," she said. He could understand that. His mother was no picnic and he had more than his fair share of nightmares about her over his life.

"My mom had schizophrenia and eventually she killed herself. I feel like it was my fault. If I had done more or tried harder maybe I would have seen the signs. Maybe I could have saved her life," Lucy said. Brandon turned his hand over and gave hers a squeeze.

"I'm sorry. That's rough," he said. "My dad died when I was a kid. He didn't kill himself but I know how tough the loss of a parent can be," Brandon added. Lucy smiled and wiped her eyes.

"Listen. We can reschedule tonight if you need to," she said, and he shook his head. The last thing he wanted to do was sit in his basement all night.

"No. It's fine I'm looking forward to it," he said, and she smiled again.

"Me too," Lucy said, and looked down at the table. Their hands were still clasped but neither one made any move to let go.

"Why don't we take the rest of our lunch outside? Let's get you some air," she said.

"Sounds good to me," he said. The break room was starting to feel small as more people came in, and he was concerned one of his coworkers would see right through him as if he had a big, flashing neon sign on his head that said: ASK ME ABOUT THE BODY IN MY BASEMENT. He put his head down and followed her to the door while his thoughts returned to the dead woman waiting for him at home, and her dead blue eyes.

Brandon removed the bandage on Jennifer's wrist and tried to remember if he had taken his medication this morning. He quickly forgot as he looked for signs of infection and admired his stitchwork. He didn't think his stitchwork was too bad for someone who hadn't known the first thing about sewing a couple months ago.

He redressed her wrist and looked over at the table where the dead woman now laid wrapped in a blanket. Covering her had been the first thing he did when he got home. He couldn't take her eyes on him anymore. Eyes, which had clouded over while he was at work, and yet he could still feel her vacant stare penetrating him through their cloudy haze. He didn't know how Jennifer could stand being here all day with the woman looking at her. Then again as he knew from experience, Jennifer's ignoring game was God tier. He finished up by checking and redressing the bandages on her back.

"What is this get together for again?" Jennifer asked.

"Promotion opportunity," Brandon said, and was caught off guard by not only how easily the lie had rolled off his lips, but also by the fact that he didn't mind lying to her at all. It was the complete opposite of how he felt about lying to Lucy earlier.

There was something going on between them. He didn't know what it was yet, but he was feeling less guilty about wanting to find out. Anytime he thought of Lucy a warm sensation spread through his body and he got butterflies in his stomach. He tried to think of the last time Jennifer gave him that feeling and came up with nothing. Still, he knew it was wrong to pursue another woman while already being in a relationship. If he was truly unhappy, why not just leave? *Because you don't like confrontation.* Brandon thought to himself. He knew a breakup between him and Jennifer would be terribly bad. She would guilt him and throw the fire in his face again. *What's the alternative? Are you going to just date them both forever? Eventually you'll have to make a choice.*

"The stitching and the skin all look good. I don't know how long the meeting is going to be and then I have the body to take care of. Don't wait up," he said, and almost gave her a small peck on the cheek like he always did any time he left the house and changed his mind.

"Bye," he said without a look back, and walked out the door. He hoped it would get to her and make her question why but he knew better. If he wasn't around she didn't think about him at all.

Anxiety flooded Brandon's body. The *click-click* of his turn signal sounded like someone banging on a bass drum in his ears. He rubbed his sweaty palms against the steering wheel as his heart trip hammered in his chest. Was he really going to go on a date with a dead body in his trunk? He had to be crazy. He knew he should have taken Lucy up on her offer to do it another night, but he let his excitement get the best of him.

He couldn't help it, being with Lucy came so easy. It amazed him how quick and how close they became after the awkwardness in Jerry's office on her first day. She got him in a way no one else ever had. He felt so right with her like he was a hand and she was a perfectly sized glove. His relationship with Jennifer had never been this good, not even the beginning of it when couples experienced the honeymoon phase. Looking back on it now he should have known then.

Brandon drove down the busy street lined with bars and restaurants on both sides until he came to the designated pay parking lot at the end of the block and pulled in. He went to the back of the lot and backed into an empty space so the back of his car was against the red, bricked building sitting on the other edge of the parking lot. Putting the trunk, and the body against the building made him feel better, he didn't know why. He walked to the front of the lot and paid the attendant in the booth enough money for five hours. Brandon didn't think the date would go on that long but he wanted to give himself as much time as possible. It would be a bad night if his car was towed and impounded with a dead body in the trunk.

He walked down the heavily congested sidewalk cutting through the throng of people. Some were smokers stepping out of establishments to get their fix. While others were migrating from one bar or restaurant to another. Loud music pulsed in the night from the concert venue on the corner. The city was always alive on a Friday night, even during a pandemic. He found Lucy already waiting for him outside the Tequila Cowboy and lost his breath. This was the first time he was seeing her in anything other than her work uniform and she looked amazing even if she was only wearing a horror movie t-shirt and blue jeans.

The blue jeans hugged her hips and showed off the shape of her legs while the black Night of the Living Dead t-shirt hung a little loose but not as loose as her work shirt. He could see hints of the shape beneath it. She had curled her hair and it looked like tight ringlets of fire.

"Hey!" He called out. She found him and smiled as he ran across the street. Lucy hugged him as soon as he stepped onto the curb and again she smelled like vanilla. It made him lightheaded and took him back to his days as a lovesick teenager. He thought of the girl he had a crush on in high school for the first time in years. Nicole Bennett, her name came forth in his mind. Brandon saw himself sitting on the swing set in his backyard looking at her picture in the yearbook while he listened to the Gin Blossoms on his portable CD player. He was six years post-accident by then and the effects were becoming more evident.

"I was starting to think you weren't coming," she said.

"Not a chance. I like your shirt," he said, and lead her inside.

The bar was dimly lit and the smell of sweat and alcohol hung on the air. Brandon leaned against a brick column while Lucy sucked at her long island iced tea with a straw. Across from them a small, obviously drunk woman clung to a mechanical bull for dear life while pop music blared from the speakers placed around the enclosed space.

"Ooh I like this song let's dance," Lucy said.

"Oh no. I don't dance," Brandon said as she drug him away from the mechanical bull toward the dance floor.

"This is not a good idea," he said. Lucy put her arms around his neck.

"It's a ballad. Put your hands on my hips and sway,"

"Alright but when I injure somebody it's on you," he said.

"I'm sure you'll be fine," she said. They swayed in place to the rhythm of the music. Lucy moved her arms from around his neck to around his waist and laid her head on his chest. The smell of her mint shampoo mixed with the vanilla and created an intoxicating scent. She looked up at him and his heart thudded. Her green eyes stared into his and he thought for sure she could see all the way into his soul. None of his secrets were safe from her including the woman he had killed. She would be able to see it all. Lucy brought her face up to his and before he could make himself stop he leaned his head down and their lips met.

His heart exploded and time stood still. The music dulled as if it were coming from somewhere else and to Brandon it felt like he and Lucy were not only the only two people on the dance floor, but the only two in the world. He pulled her in by her hips and he heard her breath hitch. Thoughts of Jennifer tried to crowd in but he deftly swatted them away. He couldn't remember the last time he felt the way he was feeling now. Content. He put one hand in her hair and grabbed it. He tugged on it as he increased the pressure on her lips.

"Do you want to get out of here?" He asked.

"I'll go anywhere you want to go," she said.

"I have something I want to show you. Follow me," he said, and lead her off the dance floor.

—SEVEN—

Brandon waited for Lucy to get out of her car before taking her hand and leading her along the concrete walkway of the Mount Washington Overlook. The end of the walkway gave way to a huge, concrete circle. A black metal rail encircled the whole disc. He walked her to the railing and she gasped.

The concrete pad was built into the top of the hill, supported by two cylindrical columns. The hill sloped downward beneath them at a steep angle. They looked across the river where the Pittsburgh skyline dominated the night sky. In the foreground two yellow bridges passed in front of the city on each side forming a triangle with the fountain that sat on the bank of the river. It's water shot high in the air. Lucy looked at him and her eyes twinkled with the reflection of the city lights.

"I have no words," she said.

"This is my place. I like to come up here and stare at the city while I think," he said. Lucy turned her attention back to the view.

"It's absolutely stunning,"

"I need to tell you something," he said.

"What?"

Brandon stared at the city running over what he wanted to say in his head. Also, he was enjoying the last good minutes of their time together as he knew what he was about to say was going to ruin everything.

"I shouldn't have kissed you in the bar. I have a girlfriend and even though things have been wrong between us for a long time it still doesn't excuse it," he said.

"I know," Lucy said, and Brandon didn't know how to react. He had expected anger, screaming, or at the least her leaving without another word, giving him a reproachful look as she went.

"What?" He finally managed to ask.

"People at work talk. The girlfriend, the fire, I know about all of it and if you want me to back off or wait we can. There is something between us. My life was not the greatest before taking this job but now I look forward to getting up and going to work because I know I'm going to see you," she said.

"Is it because of what happened to your mom?" He asked, and Lucy nodded.

"No matter how many times I tell myself there was nothing I could do to save her. I still think I could have and blame myself. It's not like I could force her to take her meds,"

"It's the same thing with me and Jennifer. I wasn't home the night of the fire and she got burned. Even though part of me knows it isn't my fault I still blame myself. It doesn't help that she also blames me," he said.

"Wait. She has told you she blames you?" Lucy asked.

"Many times,"

"I'm sorry. That is messed up. That's the last thing you need to hear when you already feel guilty," she said. Brandon looked down at the river and watched a barge go by, disturbing the once peaceful water and causing the reflection of the lights to ripple and bounce on the waves. Inside he felt the same as the churning water only it was his thoughts and feelings bouncing around.

"I'm ending things with her though," he said, and smiled. "You're right about there being something between us and I want to see where it goes. When I get home tonight I'm going to tell her I'll help her get on her feet again but the relationship is over. It has been for a long time," he added. What he left unsaid was what getting Jennifer back on her feet would entail. He had to get one more body. Lucy took his hand in hers.

"Can I ask you something?" She asked.

"Anything," he said.

"I don't want to offend you but sometimes you act like or say things that remind me of my mother, are you schizophrenic?" She asked.

"I am, but I take my medicine," he lied. She hugged him and when they broke their embrace he pushed one of her red ringlets out of her face as a small breeze blew around the overlook. They stared into each other's eyes and for the second time tonight their lips met, lightly at first and then building in intensity. Brandon felt bad lying about the medicine but it wouldn't be a lie long he told himself. He decided right here and now he would be more vigilant about taking his medication. There was nothing he wouldn't do to have Lucy in his life. He smiled; everything was about to change.

After saying goodbye to Lucy at the overlook, Brandon drove his car north out of the city. He drove past the big, blue, steel bridge connecting Sewickley to Route 51 on the other side of the river.

A few minutes later he turned down a tight, little dirt trail lined with a small section of trees on each side and crossed over a set of train tracks before coming into a dirt clearing. He guided his car across the clearing and came to a stop at the edge of the river.

He got out of the car and climbed up on the front hood where he sat and looked at the water. There was nothing out here except him and the stars this time of night. He found solitude in the darkness and felt hidden and safe. His body was still on fire from Lucy's touch. He could still smell her mixture of vanilla and mint while the ghost of her kiss still lingered on his lips. Brandon watched the river roll by in its smooth, sloshing current. Before tonight he would have considered jumping in the river and letting the current carry him wherever it may. Somewhere far from Jennifer and far from here but not now. For the first time in a long time he felt good, like everything was going to be alright. He jumped down, went around to the back of the car, and popped the trunk.

The two little lights in the trunk illuminated the dead woman's face. All the driving had caused the blanket he wrapped her in to fall open, and now her cloudy, icy blue eyes stared at him accusingly. His chest tightened and his heart stopped for a moment. He was suddenly a hundred percent sure he had made a mistake. The woman, whomever she had been, had been human all along. *Maybe she doesn't have the scary face anymore because she's dead. You killed whatever evil was inside of her. You set her free.* Brandon tried to reassure himself but he wasn't so sure.

He didn't have time to think about it. It was getting late and he needed to get moving. He grabbed the trash bag of bloody items and threw it into the river. When he was done he came back for the body. He pulled her out of the trunk as gently as possible. *What are you being gently now for? A little late now isn't it?* He thought and ignored the voice in his head. He rolled the body to the edge of the river and pushed it in with his foot. The body hit the water with a tiny splash and floated away in the darkness.

Brandon climbed back in the car and headed for home lighter in spirit. Only one more and then he could cut Jennifer lose and begin the life he was always meant to have. A life with Lucy.

Brandon stood in the kitchen and downed his medicine with one gulp of water. *Here's to day one.* He thought to himself and sat the empty glass in the sink. The first step to a new him was complete. The hardest part, however, was still coming. The conversation with Jennifer. He had been so worn out after the date and the dumping of the body last night he didn't have the energy to do it then.

He turned from the sink ready to go downstairs and get the fight out of the way when he realized he'd been upstairs for a good ten minutes and hadn't heard a single word from his mother. It wasn't like her to let him take his medication in peace. If he was upstairs then she had something to say.

"Maybe she's dead," a voice came from behind him. He turned around and jumped back from the counter.

"What the fuck!" He hissed as the back of his head hit against the refrigerator. He put his hand against the back of his head feeling for wetness when his vision changed.

He was no longer in the kitchen. Instead, he was lying underwater, struggling to sit up, someone was holding him down. He tried to pull himself up but his hands slid against the white porcelain walls of the bathtub and the back of his head throbbed.

Seconds or minutes later, he had no way of knowing, Brandon was back in the dirty, dim lit kitchen, gasping for breath. He looked at the counter and the thing that had scared him was still there.

"Yeah. I'm back asshole," she said. It was the woman he killed. She sat on the counter. A musky smell of fish and soil filled the kitchen. The purple skirt and black shirt she wore were soaked with water and clung to her pale skin. She looked at him with milky colored clouded eyes.

"No, no," he said, and shook his head. "You're not real. You can't be here," he added and staggered back making sure to avoid the refrigerator this time. She slid off the counter and he heard the water squish in her shoes when her feet hit the floor.

"Well not anymore. You saw to that yourself didn't you?" She asked, and dirty, mud-stained teeth peeked at him from behind her dark, blue lips. She grabbed the bottom of her shirt and wrung it out sending water dripping all over the kitchen floor. She shambled toward him like a zombie, her arms, and legs stiff. Brandon saw Lucy and her Night of the Living Dead t-shirt from last night and easily stepped around the woman. He closed his eyes and rubbed them like he had that day in the car as the woman tried to turn back toward him in a wide circle. *It's alright. Count to three and when you open your eyes she'll be gone.* He told himself. He counted and opened his eyes to find her still there.

"Why are you still here?" He asked.

"I'm haunting you," she said.

"No. I don't have time for this. I'm trying to put my life back together here," he said.

"And I was trying to live mine," she shot back. He ignored her and went to the living room. His mother still hadn't said anything and he was beginning to think something was wrong. No way would she listen to him having a conversation in the kitchen and not try to insert herself.

He walked into the darkened living room to find the television on but turned down. His mother was lying still in her hospital style bed in the middle of the room. Other than the television it was the only other thing in the room. All the other furniture had to go to accommodate the bed. He remembered the day he moved the furniture out and how all his mother had done was complain. He was being too rough with it. He was going to break it. After twenty minutes of her constant haranguing he had wanted to throw the furniture and break it on purpose while screaming who gives a fuck. Once it left the living room it was never going to be used again anyway. If there was one thing Maryanne Ross had been good at that wasn't cleaning it was browbeating her son. He hated it and yet somehow managed to pick a woman in Jennifer, who picked up right where his mother had left off in bringing him to heel.

Brandon stared at his mother, looking for the rise and fall of her chest that would tell him she was alive. A few moments later he saw it and a small feeling of disappointment stole over his heart. *You could do it yourself.* She wasn't mobile anymore and her mind was slipping hence the hospital bed in the first place. She might as well be a defenseless child for all the resistance she would be able to put up. He balled his hands into fists and took a step toward the bed before stopping himself. He couldn't hurt her, the whole reason he had moved back home was to take care of her. A fact that had displeased his uncle to no end. When Brandon pressed him as to the reasons why it upset him he shut down and refused to elaborate, instead, telling him to do whatever he wanted but to be careful.

"When are you going to get me more skin?" Jennifer asked the minute he came down the stairs. The question instantly set him on edge.

"I literally just killed someone two days ago," he said. "Like, are you serious right now?" He asked her and sat down on the bed to put on his boots. He didn't know why he was getting mad at her for starting a fight. A fight would make what he had to say easier. It was another instance of her being ungrateful which only reinforced his decision.

"I should have known you would wimp out after one body. That's what you do. Wimp out," she spat at him. Brandon finished with his boots and stood up, a small smile spreading across his face. This was the moment of truth. It was finally time for him to take her down a peg.

"You know there are these people known as police right? I would honestly love to get you a body as soon as possible because once I do we're done,"

"There will be no nitpicking. I don't care if there are scars or tattoos or anything. You get what you get and then you're getting out," he said, and waited for her response. His chest heaving.

"Works for me. I'm tired of being stranded in this basement with you being the only person who knows I exist. Finally I can find a real man," Jennifer shot back. *Just finish the job you started the other night and kill her instead. Why let her pull you in deeper?* For the second time this morning, Brandon found his hands curling into fists and thoughts of murder running through his mind. What was stopping him? The first one was the hardest and it was already out of the way. He walked toward her and she flinched backward, and part of him enjoyed seeing her afraid.

"I'm going to work," he said, and walked past her. He wrenched the crooked wooden door open and walked out without looking back, leaving her to either wallow in pity or be happy they were splitting. At this point he didn't care which. Now that his intentions were out in the open Brandon felt as if a huge weight had been lifted off his chest. He was one more step closer to being with Lucy and the life he was supposed to have.

He found the dead woman leaning against the front of his car waiting for him when he came outside. She looked worse in the daylight than she had in the dark kitchen. Brandon could now see her shirt and skirt was also caked with mud, as was her hair.

"You cut off my tattoo and put it on that thing in the basement?" She asked, and he ignored her. He climbed in the car and backed out of the driveway without replying. He wasn't going to engage with a figment of his imagination. That way lied madness.

—EIGHT—

Brandon drove to work feeling fine. The sun was out and he had the window down. Nothing was getting to him today, not even the business with the dead woman in his kitchen. A small part of him worried about the things he had been seeing. The eyeless women with the flies and now a walking, talking corpse but he was under a lot of stress lately. Maybe he was having night terrors while awake. Was that possible? He wasn't sure. He wasn't a psychologist but it sounded plausible. *Or maybe your mom passed some of her madness on to you.* The old familiar voice said in his head. Brandon ignored it. He was sure it was the stress and once the stressors were removed from his life he would be fine.

"Good riddance to bad rubbish," he said aloud, and drove up to the plant's gate where he had to show his ID badge to the guard before being waived through. He pulled into an empty space and smiled when he saw Lucy's forest green SUV parked a couple of spaces down. He couldn't wait to see her, even with everything that had happened at home this morning he still had a little high from their date last night.

Brandon walked down the long white hallway past Jerry's office toward the breakroom and he saw a crowd of people gathered and knew something was wrong. The breakroom was usually deserted at the start of shift. People only stopped long enough to clock in and put their lunches in the refrigerator before heading to their assigned stations.

"Have you seen this?" Lucy asked him when he came in and found her with everyone else in front of the television. He looked at the screen and his stomach flipped on itself. There was a picture of the woman he killed on the screen. She was smiling and wearing a gold and blue Pitt University sweater. Her brown hair was pulled up in a high ponytail.

"...she hasn't been seen in two days. Friends say she was going out Tuesday night and she never showed up for class Wednesday or Thursday. Her parents reported her missing this morning. She has a galaxy tattoo on her inner right wrist. If anyone has any information regarding the disappearance of Sarah Mason they are encouraged to contact the police. In other news..." the newscaster went on and the breakroom spun around Brandon. He leaned forward and put a hand on the closest table to steady himself and tried not to draw attention. A million thoughts rattled around inside his head, and he was sure the second someone looked at him they would see the guilt written on his face. *You should have been prepared for this. It's fine. You took steps. There were no witnesses. You got rid of all the evidence.* All of it except the tattoo currently stitched to Jennifer's wrist.

"Oh yeah. You're fucked," he looked up to see the dead woman, Sarah, staring at him from where she sat in one of the empty chairs. Her skin had gone paler and started cracking since he saw her this morning. She stood up from the chair and her movement had become smoother, but still slightly jerky. *She's not here. She isn't real.* Brandon pulled himself together and made a hasty exit from the breakroom.

"I was wondering where you had gone off to," Lucy said. Brandon stood at the beginning of the gravel walkway to go around the perimeter. The weather was beautiful, the sun hung high in the sky with little wind. It did nothing to improve his mood as he saw Lucy wasn't alone. Sarah, the undead specter, shuffled next to her. A grotesque smile painted on her decaying face.

How was he supposed to enjoy the day when a dead woman was following him around? He looked at the river and his mind returned to last night when he had pushed her lifeless body into this same river around thirteen miles give or take downstream.

"I had fun last night," Lucy said.

"Me too," Brandon said a little noncommittally. He couldn't take his eyes off of Sarah's moldering corpse and the pungent aroma of fish and soil made his eyes water. She smiled at him and a millipede slithered between her mud-stained teeth and down over her lower lip. He shuddered and quickly looked away.

"Yeah. Sounds like it," Lucy said and he heard the hurt in her voice.

"I'm sorry," he said and took her hand. Lucy looked around to see if they were being watched, but he didn't care if they were.

"I'm just having a day," he said.

"Wait. You killed me and cut off a piece of my skin for someone you're not even being faithful to!" Sarah yelled at him and he did his best to ignore her. The next thing he knew he was being pelted with gravel. He flinched away and Lucy looked at him puzzled.

"Sorry I thought I saw a bee," he said, and tried harder to ignore the restless rock slinging spirit now riding shotgun in his life.

"What's going on? Why are you having a day?" Lucy asked.

"Just thinking about my dad," Brandon said pulling something out of midair. He couldn't tell her the real reason. He couldn't tell her he was being haunted by the woman he killed. The same woman the whole breakroom saw on the news a couple minutes ago.

"Not a good relationship? I get it, my relationship with my dad is super strained," she said.

"My dad was my best friend. He died when I was a kid," he said, and stared across the river. The water going by reminded him a lot of himself in that moment. It looked calm on the surface but there were all kinds of things going on beneath in the places where eyes couldn't see.

"I remember you said he passed away," Lucy said.

"He was everything I wish I could be. He was blessed with an infinite well of patience. He would always answer my questions and we used to sit at the kitchen table and build Legos. He had this old school radio. A cheap little, black plastic thing. Anyway we would sit there and listen to the classic rock channel while we built. The Beatles, The Rolling Stones, Led Zeppelin, those were his favorites," Brandon said.

"Oh boo hoo my daddy died. If you want to be sad about something be sad about being a murderer!" Sarah said and stomped her foot. Her knee buckled inward with a sickening crack and her left leg canted at a 45-degree angle with the ground. She looked at him, a look of surprise etched into the pale countenance of her face. He watched as she grabbed her knee with both hands and tried to pull it back into place.

"Come on. Let's finish our rounds," he said seeing a chance to lose his zombified stalker. He put his arm around Lucy's shoulders and led her down the walkway.

"I was thinking we should have dinner next time. How would you feel about coming to my place sometime?" She asked.

"I would like that a lot," he said.

"Don't you walk away from me!" Sarah yelled after him but the farther away they got the less he could hear her.

Brandon tried to pinpoint the exact moment his life went wrong as he cleaned and redressed Jennifer's bandages while she sat in front of the television. Was it the day his head got cracked in an accident he couldn't remember? Maybe it was when his father died. Boys needed their fathers after all and his had been taken from him at an early age. They had been two peas in a pod and he had preferred his father to his mother even then. The two of them had formed a special club she had never been able to penetrate.

He finished and looked around the run-down basement, the claustrophobic space that smothered him just as much as the woman he shared the space with and the other one that resided upstairs. Brandon thought another change was in order. Once Jennifer was gone that was it for this basement. He would move out and get his own space. A space above ground where he would be able look outside and feel the sun on his face. As for taking care of his mother, she could go to a home. It was time for him to actually live his life.

"I was going to wait until we were finished to tell you but I've met someone," Brandon said. He hadn't been planning to tell her now but it just came out. Jennifer never turned her attention away from the television.

"Good for you," she said in a bored, distracted tone and he considered striding across the basement and kicking the screen in. He saw it in his mind. He heard the crunch of the glass as the spiderweb crack spread across the screen before it gave way and buckled inward under the heel of his boot and the sparks as the picture tube inside blew. The thought of it gave him a savage pleasure because he knew it would hurt her and he was tired of being ignored. The need to be spiteful and purposefully cause someone pain he knew came from his mother.

His whole body crackled with the need to do it and he had a tough time seeing why he shouldn't. Jennifer had never passed up an opportunity to hurt him over the years without thinking twice about it. In fact he was sure she enjoyed it. He started toward the television she loved so much and looked at her out of the side of his eye as he went past and received a nasty jolt.

Jennifer still sat in the recliner but she was dead. The skin he had sewn to her hung loosely against her burned, decayed skin. His mouth went dry and his heart sped up in his chest. She couldn't be dead; she had spoken to him not more than five seconds ago. He stopped, his plan to destroy the television forgotten and grabbed her instead.

"Ow! What is wrong with you? Why do you like to hurt me?" She cried. She wasn't dead, again he was seeing things.

The basement swam in front of him and he dropped down on the bed. He squeezed his head between his hands and stared down at the floor. What in the hell was going on? He took three slow steadying breaths and laid back on the bed closing his eyes. He didn't know what was going on but everything was fine.

Everything is not fine.

Brandon ignored the voice in his head and concentrated on calming down. He thought of Lucy. He pictured running his hands through her red hair and smelling her vanilla scent. He held her smiling face in his mind and calmed down. He rolled onto his side and opened his eyes to see Sarah's slowly rotting corpse staring at him, her face only inches from his. He jumped up off the bed and stumbled into the little wooden table he had killed her on sending it sliding a couple of feet where it banged against the wall with a hollow clap.

"Jesus Christ!"

"What?" Sarah asked as she sat up and smiled at him without breaking eye contact. "What are you afraid of? Unlike you, I can't hurt anybody," she said. Brandon sat down on the edge of the table and put his head in his hands. It was finally happening. His mother had passed whatever was wrong with her down to him after all.

—NINE—

The body floated on its back, bobbing up and down lazily on the current. Each gentle rise and fall of the water pushed the body against the small outcropping of rocks that had stopped it from floating on down the river.

A morning drizzle pelted off Detective Genevieve Wurtz' black umbrella as she made her way down to the rocks where her partner already stood. She had known the day was going to be shit as soon as she woke up to the dark clouds this morning. Still, she had assumed it would be normal shit and not body floating in the river shit.

The crowd had already gathered by time she arrived. Humans, much like vultures had an attraction for the dead.

"What have we got?" She asked as she looked down at the woman's pale face. Cloudy eyes stared lifelessly past her at the gray sky. The only deviation of color or lack thereof in her milky skin were her lips, which were a dark shade of blue. She looked over the body but her attention kept coming back to the woman's dead blue eyes. Emptiness filled Genevieve's heart as she watched them fill with rain.

She hated floaters, especially in this town. The waterways around Pittsburgh had a propensity for turning up bodies which lead to conspiracy theories about serial killers. People didn't seem to understand that when you have a large populace near water you were going to have bodies in the water from time to time. Once the discovery of the body hit the news the nutters would be out in full force. She had a couple weeks of people blowing their phone lines up all day with hot tips to look forward to.

Fuck. She sighed and looked off down the river and her eyes were drawn to the baby blue steel bridge that spanned the waterway. The bridge she had driven over herself to get here. Underneath the cement support poles were covered in graffiti. Multiple smiley faces drawn in runny spray paint stared back at her.

"You don't recognize her?" Her partner asked. Clive was fifteen years older than her and had one foot out the door into retirement. Genevieve studied the woman again and found she did recognize her. It was the missing girl from the news.

"Son of a bitch," she said.

"Yep. No cause of death yet obviously or signs of trauma other than the wrist," Clive said.

"What's with the wrist?" She asked.

"Her tattoo is gone," he said. If her tattoo was gone that meant this was done on purpose. *Who hurt you?* Genevieve thought. She didn't want to get too far ahead of herself. There were still too many questions that needed answers. How long had she been dead? Was she dead before she hit the water? How long had she been out here? She climbed off the rocks and climbed the bank as the Medical Examiner and his assistant struggled to wheel their gurney through the crowd and the wet grass.

"Give em some room," Genevieve said, and the crowd parted but didn't leave. She looked back down at the floating woman's body rising and falling on the sloshing water and the rain chilled her to the bone. Sometimes she hated this world and thought the dead were better off than those who were left behind until she remembered she'd have to sit the woman's parents down today and tell them what happened to their daughter.

"Who found her?" Genevieve asked as Clive made his way off the rocks and joined her on the shore. He pointed to an older man standing in the front of the crowd with a black dog on a leash.

"Found her while taking his dog on a morning walk," he said.

"Think he'll be able to tell us anything?"

"Outside of finding her probably not. People dump bodies in a river so they float away. If she was put in here she'd be floating through Ohio by now not placed in between the rocks. No, I think she was put in somewhere upstream closer to the city. Probably last night," Clive said. She knew he was right but due diligence dictated they speak with old man anyway. She sighed, she wanted nothing more than to get out of the rain.

"Sir do you live close to here?" She pointed at the older man with the dog as she crossed the open space between them.

"Down around the bend there," the older man said and pointed back upstream where the flowing river disappeared around a long sloping bend.

"Why don't we give you and your dog a ride and you can tell us what you saw this morning?" Clive escorted the man through the crowd while she turned back to the river. The M.E. had the body loaded onto the gurney and one pale arm flopped out of the not quite closed body bag and hung down as they tried to wheel the gurney off the rocks.

Jesus. Genevieve thought as she watched the brownish water flow lazily by. She stared transfixed by its smooth up and down movement. What secrets was it keeping in its murky depths?

Streetlights painted lighted halos on the sidewalks of East Liberty as Brandon stalked Penn Avenue. The warm night air coming in through his open car window felt good against his skin. Summer was finally here and his freedom was close at hand.

Night covered everything the lights didn't touch and the shadows held dark things. The neighborhood he cruised through had a reputation. Assaults, murders, drugs, prostitution, it was a one stop shop for crime. Seeing Sarah's picture on the news had given him a fright and he knew he had to pick his last victim more carefully. He had to pick somebody no one was going to miss. Someone the police wouldn't bother to look for and every serial killer documentary he had ever seen told him a prostitute would check both of those boxes. While this fact had revolted him as a viewer, in this case he was hoping to use the broken system to get one last kill.

He watched the people walking along the sidewalks and thought about a different kind of story now. The one last job stories that always went sideways. Did he really need to do one more? He was already cutting Jennifer loose did it really matter if he killed one more person for her or not? *It's the least you could do. You let her get burned. At least this way you leave the relationship even.*

"You are obsessed with that fire aren't you?" He looked over to see Sarah riding shotgun in the passenger seat. The car filled with the smell of rotting flesh and her skin was no longer pale. It had taken on a sickly greenish tint. Her cloudy eyes sat far back in deep black sockets. She smiled at him and her teeth were rotted.

"What happened to you?" Brandon asked.

"You did,"

"No. I mean, you didn't look like this earlier," he turned his head toward the open window and took deep breaths of fresh air, his eyes watering.

"I'm decaying. It happens when you die," she said.

"Why won't you leave me alone?" Brandon asked and turned his attention back to the road and sidewalks where people walked, completely oblivious to the fact a predator was among them, waiting for one of them to make a mistake or go off on their own so he would have an opening.

"You're seeing me because you feel guilty. You feel guilty about killing me the same way you feel guilty about the fire. The funny thing is you should really only feel guilty about me, because while you did kill me you didn't set the fire," she said.

"I might as well have," he said.

"How so? You were at work. It's not like you lied about where you were at or were out doing something you weren't supposed to. It was an accident," she said.

"I'm sorry I killed you," Brandon said, and wiped away the tears running down his face. He knew she wasn't real and that he would never be able to apologize to the actual Sarah but it was the best he could do.

Brandon turned off the main road and shot down a side street as he drove in a circle so he could cruise the block again. He looked at the radio clock. Its neon green numbers looked like they were glowing in the dark. It was getting late but he couldn't go home empty handed. He wanted to get all of this done and over with.

"Just because I'm not real doesn't mean I can't give you helpful advice. I'm kicking around inside your head," she said, and a light went off in his head, bright and fast. He couldn't remember when he had a thought with such clarity. If she existed only in his mind then she was in there with the jumbled thoughts and memories of his accident. Could he use her to retrieve them from the darkened areas of his mind like a dead librarian for dead memory files?

"Do you know anything about my accident?" He asked her.

"Talk to your uncle," she said.

"I've tried that,"

"When you were a child. You're an adult now. Make him tell you," she said. Brandon turned back onto the main road and found what he was looking for a corner up.

The woman stood by the corner under the streetlight wearing red spaghetti strap shirt and black skirt with a pair of black heels. The two of them locked eyes and he saw she looked like Jennifer with her slightly curly, shoulder length blonde hair. She started toward the car as he pulled over to the curb.

"Again. You don't have to do this," Sarah said.

"I know you think that but I do," he said and she disappeared as the woman came up to the window and leaned her head in.

"Looking for a date?" She asked.

"Yeah. Climb in," he said. The woman got in the car and he pulled away. He drove down the street and turned off into a secluded alley way between two buildings.

Brandon drove halfway down the alley and pulled in next to a battered dumpster. He turned toward the woman and watched as the sockets around her eyes grew large and black as her eyes disappeared. Her mouth started to go slack and he knew he had to act quick. He slid across the seat and wrapped his hands around her throat. She fought back, kicking, and clawing but there was nowhere for her to go in the tight quarters of the front seat. He saw Jennifer's face as he choked the life from her. He squeezed as hard as he could and felt her windpipe break beneath his hands. The woman's body went limp and Brandon panted from exhaustion. Still, the hard part was done and he was another step closer to being free. He took a moment to catch his breath and steady himself before he started the car and disappeared into the night as if he'd never been there at all.

Brandon wiped the sweat from his brow with the back of his hand which was slick with blood and sweat. He stood over the flayed body of the prostitute lying on the plastic on the table. Strips of skin varying in length hung from the clothesline above the table. The smell of her blood filled the small basement and he did his best not to gag.

"I think that is it," he said and went to the small sink in the corner and washed his hands. Jennifer said nothing, she only stared at the skin hanging from the line and he watched her, waiting for her to make the smallest complaint. If she did she would be out the door right now. *Do you think it's a good idea to just let her go? What if she tells someone? You should kill her too. It's the best way to make the break completely clean.* He couldn't do that. If he killed her too then he killed two other women for no reason. Also she couldn't tell anyone as she would be an accessory. The evidence would literally be her body.

He returned to the table and wrapped the body in the plastic. This time he wasn't going to hold on to the body for two days. He'd put it in the trunk and go dump it while he waited for the skin to dry. When he returned he would sew the skin together and put it on Jennifer's body all at once. No more sewing it on piece by piece.

"We finish this tonight. You then get a week to heal and then you're out. I never want to see you again," Brandon said. Jennifer nodded as he picked the woman's body up and carried it out the door.

—TEN—

Detective Wurtz rode the elevator down to the basement of the hospital. She hated hospitals and their general antiseptic odor. She didn't like the stories hospitals tried to tell with their white walls, floors, and cleaners. They tried to pass themselves off as places of healing but in her experience all hospitals were filled with nothing but death. It furtively sloughed beneath the smell of cleanliness while people smiled at you and told you everything would be fine.

She waited on the elevator to finish its slow descent to the basement where they kept the dead. She had arrived at work this morning to a message on her desk from the medical examiner stating the autopsy on the floater, Sarah Mason, was complete and he had some preliminary findings for her. She stared at the elevator doors and the grimy, stainless steel distorted her reflection. She looked wavy and melted like the screaming person in that famous Munch painting. She tried to remember what it was called but the name escaped her. The elevator stopped with a ding and the doors slid open.

Genevieve stepped into the hallway and scrunched her nose. The antiseptic smell followed her even down here but unlike upstairs a sour smell mixed in with it below the surface. She walked down the hall and her boots squeaked on the white linoleum floor with every step she took. It sounded like she was playing basketball in the gym instead of walking to the morgue. She reached the heavy double doors at the end of the hall and pushed them open.

"Good morning detective. Where is your partner?" He asked in his soft German accent as he looked up from the paperwork on his desk. She tried to remember the last time she had seen Clive come to the morgue as the doors swung shut behind her. *I don't hang out with dead people. I hunt their killers.* She heard his voice in her head. He had uttered that nonsensical comment seven years and one small affair between them ago. She knew sleeping with her partner made her a cliché but it was only a couple of times and there was something about his combination of gruffness and aloofness she liked. Genevieve didn't know if they had been in love or if it would have gone that far because she ended it quickly. She would never be taken seriously if she was sleeping with her older partner and Genevieve Wurtz had aspirations that didn't stop at Detective. She was shooting for a captaincy at the least and maybe Commissioner after that.

"I heard you've got something for me," she said, ignoring his question about where her partner was.

"Ah I do," he said, and got up from his desk. He led her over to the drawers lining the far wall and pulled the drawer with Sarah's body out. He took the sheet down to her waist and the dark stitches of her Y incision stood out in stark contrast against her skin. Skin that looked paler to Genevieve than the day they pulled her out of the river.

"Do we have a cause of death or are we waiting on toxicology for that?" She asked. Kurt drew her attention to a pair of nasty purple bruises around her throat.

"She was strangled," he said.

"No water in the lungs?" She asked and Kurt shook his head.

"She was dead long before she hit the water," he said. Between them, Sarah's empty eyes stared up at the ceiling.

"What about the arm wound?"

"Skin was definitely taken off postmortem and on purpose. The cut lines are little rough but the geometry of the cut is too measured for it not to have been intentional," he said.

"They cut off her tattoo. Do you think it was done to slow down identification?" She asked.

"Only if they don't know how identification works. No. If they were trying to hide who she was they would have taken her fingertips and teeth as well. I think whoever did this wanted the tattoo," he said.

"Like a trophy. Great," she said. The Pittsburgh has a serial killer crowd that came out anytime a body showed up in the river were going to have a field day with this.

"I have two more things for you," Kurt said. First he drew her attention to the back of Sarah's hand.

"Look at this," he said and grabbed a black light. He shined it on the back of Sarah's hand and Genevieve saw an ink stamp.

"I found it but I don't know where it's for?" Kurt said.

"That's alright. I do," she said, and took out her cellphone. She dialed Clive's number and dropped it to the floor with a loud whack as it landed face down when Kurt rolled Sarah's body over.

"The tattoo isn't all they took," Kurt said, and showed Genevieve two more spots where the skin had been removed.

"Damn it," she said, and picked up her phone. She let out a sigh of relief when she found the screen wasn't cracked. The last thing she needed was to have to find time to replace a phone. She dialed Clive's number again and waited.

"Hey. Stop what you're doing and meet me at Cavo," she said when he answered.

Forty minutes later Genevieve pulled up and parked across the street from the brown brick building with the black sign on the side that read: CAVO in big white letters. She got out of the car, popped into the small bakery across the street.

She returned to her small, black sedan with her late breakfast and coffee. She sat on the hood with her feet on the front bumper and ate while she waited for Clive to show up.

Genevieve finished the last bite of her croissant and took a swig of her coffee as Clive's dark blue, Renault Alliance turned onto Penn Avenue announcing itself with a backfire and plume of black exhaust smoke. He pulled into the empty spot along the curb in front of her and climbed out.

"That car is a menace," Genevieve said, and waved her hand back and forth trying to clear the last remnants of smoke away.

"Don't talk that way about the blue bomber. Did you get me one of those?" Clive asked and pointed at her coffee.

"Do I look like a barista, and how old is that dinosaur?" She asked pointing at his car.

"Marie here rolled off the assembly line in the glorious year of nineteen eighty-three," he said.

"Jesus. That's one year after I was born," Genevieve said.

"Really? Damn I was fifteen in eighty-three," he said and reached for her coffee. She handed it to him and watched him grimace after he took a drink. As if he had just tasted the foulest thing known to man.

"Ugh. I forgot you take yours black with not a molecule of sugar to be found," he said. She smiled and drank the rest of it. She put the empty cup and bag on the front seat of her car.

"I called the club manager after I talked to you. He's coming down to meet us," she said as they crossed the street with relative ease. During the day, the area known as the strip district was notoriously deserted. Most of the businesses lining both sides of the road were bars, night clubs, and strip clubs. The party started every night when the sun went down. For Sarah Mason that was when the party had ended.

Mitchell Ciccone, Mitch to his friends, of which he had very few was a portly man. Not fat enough to have jowls but big enough to where it looked like he had a spare tire around the bottom half of his torso. The gold rings he wore on every finger gleamed and stood out against his sun kissed skin. His slicked back, black hair was pulled up in a ponytail and he wore so much cologne he could have been classified as walking air pollution.

"What you're looking for is in the back room," he said after they exchanged pleasantries. He escorted them through the club and Genevieve took everything in with her Detective's eye.

The blue and pink neon lights were on but the dance floor was moderately lit since the shudders on the windows behind the bar were open. A young woman with black and pink hair moved around behind the bar restocking the shelves with alcohol. Music played but nowhere near the volume it would be during business hours.

"I heard about the dead woman on the news. Such a tragedy. It's unsettling that my club may be the last place she was before she died," Mitchell said as he lead them through the black door with the sign that read: EMPLOYEES ONLY. They walked down the small, carpeted hallway and he unlocked the door to the back room.

The security room was a tiny room, no bigger than a closet. A large desk sat in the middle of the room. Nine computer monitors lined the wall directly across from the front of the desk. Every monitor showed a different angle of the dancefloor and bar. Another wall to the right of the desk was taken up with what looked like huge, black computer towers with blinking lights.

"These are all of our servers. We archive all of our footage. As far as how to retrieve something specific for you I have no idea. My security guy Tony is on the way," he said.

"He's already here," they all turned around to find Tony standing in the doorway. A younger looking guy with thick, but well-groomed black facial hair and dark eyes.

Genevieve found him pleasant to look at but she quickly walled that off. She was here on business not pleasure.

"Welcome to my domain," he said as he pushed past them and sat down at the computer desk. He woke up the computer and switched one of the monitors over from being a camera feed to showing the computer's operating system.

"Give them whatever they ask for. If you all will excuse me I have other club matters needing my attention. Unless you need me to stay," Mitchell said, and looked from Genevieve to Clive like a child waiting to be told he could go.

"I think we're good for now," Genevieve said. Mitchell nodded and made himself scarce.

"Alright so what are we looking for?" Tony asked. Genevieve took out a picture of Sarah from the morgue and sat it on the desk.

"Jesus is she dead?" Tony asked.

"Yes she is. Which is why it's important we see all of the footage you have for the night of May fifteenth," Genevieve said.

"That's going to be a lot of footage," he said.

"I've got all day," she said.

"Start with feeds from the bar. I know we haven't gotten toxicology back yet but who comes to a nightclub and doesn't drink anything," Clive said.

"Will do," Tony said, and punched some keys on the keyboard. A moment later he had a bar feed on every monitor with each one showing a different hour of footage.

"There," Clive said, and pointed at the second monitor. Tony paused the feed and the three of them compared the girl on the screen to the picture on the desk.

"That's her. Let it play," Genevieve said. Tony hit the spacebar and they all watched the monitor intently. A couple minutes later a guy bumped into Sarah causing her to spill her drink and they exchanged words while he helped her clean it up. Suddenly the man looked as if he had seen something terrifying and went out onto the dance floor.

"Can you screengrab his face and print it?" Genevieve asked.

"Sure can," Tony said.

"Let's stay on the guy. Can you set up a couple monitors to follow him and keep the rest on her?" Clive asked.

"Absolutely. Let me check the timestamp at the bar and I'll pull up a feed of the dancefloor when he goes that way," Tony said. "Ok I've got him here on the dancefloor," he said.

"Is he talking to himself?" Genevieve said.

"He looks like he's having a hard time whoever he is," Clive said.

They watched him leave the dancefloor and changed the feed again to stay with him. The three of them spent the next two hours watching the man watch Sarah and then leave when she did.

"I think we found our guy," Clive said.

"Let's get back to the station. Hopefully, this guy is in the system for something and we can find out who he is," Genevieve said.

"Thank you for all your help," Clive said, and Genevieve's phone rang.

"Hello… When?.. We'll get there as soon as possible," she said and hung up.

"Station is going to have to wait. We have another body on the bank of the same river," she said.

"Where?" Clive asked.

"We're going to Ohio," she said.

—ELEVEN—

Clive navigated his ancient blue car down the thin dirt road through the woods. Genevieve looked out the window at the trees towering over both sides of the road. The sky looked like a blue crack in the foliage above.

The car shimmied and shook. Genevieve bounced up and down in her seat with every dip in the road. She put both hands on the dashboard and braced herself. The drive had taken two hours with the last thirty minutes of it being on this back road. She was all the way ready to be out of this car.

"Are we almost there?" She asked.

"Do you hear water? He said we'd know we were close when we could hear the river," Clive said. She stuck her head out the window and listened. A few minutes later she heard the faint sound of rushing water.

"I hear it. Thank Christ. Next time we take my car," she said.

They rounded a dog leg bend in the road and she saw the two police cars and a coroner's van parked just off the edge of the road. Clive pulled off into the small, grassy clearing and turned the car off. The engine stopped with a shudder.

"Seriously you need to take this car to a mechanic or better yet the junkyard," she said.

Genevieve got out of the car and found three men standing on the bank of the river, at their feet the edges of a thick piece of plastic flapped in the breeze. The three men turned around as she and Clive approached.

The sheriff was a solidly built man with short brown hair and Genevieve saw herself reflected in his aviator sunglasses. He smiled and a toothpick hung half chewed in the corner of his mouth. She noted he looked like a middle-aged Robert Urich from the old television show Spenser: For Hire.

"Sheriff Hoyt," she said and held out her hand. He ignored her and turned to Clive instead. She was used to this kind of treatment but it was still shocking when it happened. Clive stuck his hands in his pockets and the sheriff dropped his hand.

"What do you have here?" She asked pressing on. Hoyt ignored her and turned to Clive instead again.

"As you can see—," He started and Genevieve cut him off.

"Excuse me sheriff asshole. He didn't ask you I did. Now I see you might be operating as if it's still the nineteen fifties in your little backwater stretch of land here but I assure you outside of this little town time has marched on. I asked you a question and you will answer me even if your dick retreats into your body at the sight of a strong, independent woman," Genevieve said.

"Now listen here," Hoyt said and pointed his finger at her face.

"I'd stop pointing your finger at me unless you want it broken," she said. The sheriff's deputy, a man with sandy

96

blonde hair and a farmers tan saw things trending downward and approached Clive.

"You might want to do something," he said.

"Oh I am. I'm going to enjoy the show," Clive said with a smile.

"I don't know who you think you are, or what makes you think you can come into my town and talk to me like this," Hoyt said and jabbed his finger forward again.

Genevieve grabbed his finger and jammed it backwards while putting her leg behind his. Hoyt went over her leg and landed on his back. She followed him down never relinquishing her hold on his finger and put her knee in his chest. Hoyt reached for the gun on his hip and she wrenched his finger. He screamed and stopped.

"Go for it again and I'll break your finger. Are you done?" She asked and he nodded. She let go of his finger and let him up. Hoyt brushed himself off, his face flushed and sweaty.

"I'm going to file an assault charge," he said.

"No you won't because then you'd have to admit you were beat up by a woman," Genevieve said. Hoyt stalked to his car holding his finger and peeled out. She turned her attention to the deputy now.

"So you want to tell me what we got here or are we going to have a problem too?" She asked.

"No ma'am," he said.

"You alright?" Clive asked her as the deputy walked away.

"Yeah I'm fine. Bet you twenty dollars the motherfucker has a Trump sign in his front yard," she said.

The deputy lead them over to the body and opened the wet plastic. Genevieve had never seen anything like it but she kept the world's best poker face.

"She washed up this morning," he said. The woman in wrapped in plastic was completely flayed. There wasn't an inch of skin left behind.

"Christ," Clive said. Genevieve stared at the body, to go from taking a couple small pieces of skin from the first body to taking all of it with the second one was a hell of an escalation. *What in the hell is he going to do with it?* She asked herself and she wasn't sure she wanted the answer.

Brandon climbed the steps to Lucy's front porch with a bouquet of roses in his hand and a smile on his face. He had dumped the woman's body into the river a week ago now and Jennifer was mostly healed… He was free.

He knocked on the door and his heart stopped when Lucy answered. She wore a sunflower covered sundress and flats. She had styled her red hair razor straight. He tried to talk and found himself at a loss for words.

"I'll take your inability to talk as a sign that I look good," she said, and took the flowers. "Get in here," she said.

He stepped inside and waited in the front hall while she shut the door behind him. To his right the stairs ran up to the second floor. Straight ahead he saw the kitchen at the end of the hallway. Lucy headed that way with the flowers and he followed. They walked past the entrance to the living room where the television was playing.

"These are beautiful. Thank you," she said as she put water and the roses in a vase and sat it on the table.

"I have news," he said.

"Oh yeah?"

"As of today Jennifer and I are officially done so we're free to see what this could be guilt free," he said. Lucy squealed and jumped into his arms. They kissed passionately and he sat her down on the table. Their hands explored each other's bodies as they continued to go at it. Brandon's kisses left her lips and started down her neck. She grabbed his hair and wrapped her legs around his waist.

"Wait. Dinner is almost done," she said.

"To be continued," he said.

Dinner was steaks and salads they both ate quickly and he helped her clear the table and dried the dishes while she washed. Brandon stared out the window over the sink at the backyard. The setting sun covered everything in a dark orange light that made everything look as if it were on fire. A breeze blew in through the open window and he could smell the air. It had that smell that only came with the summertime. He pictured himself and Lucy lounging in that backyard or maybe chasing a kid around it someday. A little boy or little girl with her same red hair.

After the dishes they retired to the living room and sat down on the couch. The sunlight came in through the bay window behind the television casting the same orange light on the brown hardwood floors. Brandon took the room in and noted the lack of water and concrete. His basement made her living room look like the Ritz-Carlton.

"You've got a nice place here," he said. She moved from her spot and straddled his lap facing him. She wrapped her arms around his neck and smiled at him, biting her lip as she did so. She kissed him deep and slow, and nibbled at his bottom lip as she pulled back.

"Are we going to talk about my house or do you want to go upstairs?" Lucy asked him.

"Upstairs sounds great," he said. Lucy climbed off him and took him by the hand.

"Let's go," she said, and lead him toward the stairs. A moment later a news bulletin broke on the television about the second woman's body being pulled out of the river in Ohio. Neither one of them saw it.

The sun had gone down and left Lucy's room dark before they finished. Brandon laid there staring up at the ceiling with Lucy's head resting on his chest. He ran his fingers through her hair, its red color looked dulled and almost brown in the dark.

He listened to her breathing and his heart felt full. He wished he could bottle the moment and keep it forever. There were no fake, dead women, no Jennifer, no mother. There was only Lucy.

"What are you thinking about?" Her voice came to him in the dark.

"You," he said, and drifted off to sleep where he found a nightmare waiting for him.

The water of the river running behind his uncle's house was still. Brandon sat on the edge of the dock, his feet in the water, picking at the sun bleached, weathered wood with his thumbnail the same way he used to when he was a child. His looked next to him at the board he sat on and still found his and his cousin's names carved there.

The sun warmed his skin and he saw a snake slither off the opposite bank into the water. He took out his feet and sat criss cross applesauce on the dock. He wasn't a fan of snakes.

Sarah surfaced in the water below him. Her dead bloated face looked green in the sun. She smiled at him and he wanted to scream

"What's wrong? You look like you've seen a ghost," she said, and smiled wider.

"Funny," he said.

"I brought a friend," she said and the skinless body of the prostitute broke the surface of the water. Water ran from her exposed muscles in tiny, red rivulets.

"We have something to show you," Sarah said. They both grabbed him and pulled him off balance into the muddy water.

He gasped as the cold water enveloped him. He sank and tried to kick his feet to propel himself back toward the surface but his legs were too heavy. Brandon looked down and saw the two women's faces in the murky depths pulling on his legs. He kicked at them until he broke free and swam for the surface but when he broke through he was no longer in the river. He saw the white bathroom ceiling of his childhood home and his mother staring down at him.

She grimaced, her face red from exertion and planted both of her hands on his small chest. He coughed and gasped for breath as she pushed him back below the water. He clawed against the smooth, white porcelain of the bathtub and fought his way back up again to see his mother coming apart. Her normally well-kept hair had fly aways coming out of the bun. Her bangs hung in her face while the veins bulged on the side of her head. He should have been able to fight her off easily but he was no longer the big man he had grown into. He was an eight-year-old little boy again.

"God told me about your evil ways through the television this morning. He told me to send you to your daddy," she said.

"No mama. I'm not bad," Brandon said, and sucked in a deep breath before she forced him under again. He fought and the back of his head hit the bottom of the tub with a thud. The world swam in front of him but not from the water. Sharp pain exploded in the back of his head and the water around him began to turn red. He yelled out and inhaled a mouthful of water. His fighting became wild thrashes that sent water splashing everywhere as his vision started to go dark as if he were drifting backward down a long dark tunnel. Above him, the water and the bathroom ceiling were getting farther away.

He stopped fighting and his last breaths rose toward the surface of the water in slow, tiny bubbles when suddenly he was pulled from the water by a pair of bigger, stronger hands. He came out limply, sputtering and coughing, and saw his uncle's face.

His uncle lifted him from the tub and Brandon saw his mother lying on the floor cradling her bright, red cheek with her hand. She glared at them both with murderous intent.

"Come on Brandon breathe," he heard his uncle telling him while pounding on his back. Each blow sent shockwaves of pain through his body but all he could concentrate on was trying to breathe.

Brandon woke up gasping for air and found the sunlight shining in his face. He shielded his eyes with his hands and sat up. Lucy slept next to him snoring contently. He slid out from around her being careful not to wake her up. He went to the bathroom, grabbing his overnight bag on the way. He turned on the bathroom sink, cupped water in his trembling hands and took his medication.

"Two weeks," he said to his reflection in the mirror and felt sick. He had to take Sarah's advice and talk to his uncle now. He had to know if what he just dreamt was true and his uncle was the only one who could tell him.

Brandon came back to the bed and kissed her on her forehead causing her to stir.

"Hey," Lucy said, her voice still thick with sleep.

"Sorry didn't mean to wake you. I'm going to head out to my uncles. I was thinking I could come back after," he said, trying to keep his composure. He didn't want to worry her.

"Absolutely," she said propping herself up on her elbow. He leaned down and gave her a kiss.

"See you later," he said.

He didn't see her again until the end.

"I have to know. Did my mother try to kill me?" Brandon asked. His uncle took a deep breath and let it out. The two of them sat in lawn chairs on the dock and Brandon made sure to keep away from the edge after the dream he had last night.

"Finally remembered huh?" His uncle asked and took a deep drink from his bottle of beer. Brandon felt like he had been punched in the gut. The dream was true, his mother had really tried to drown him in the bathtub when he was eight years old.

"You have to understand. I loved my sister dearly but your mother wasn't right in the head," his uncle said.

"What do you mean?"

"My sister saw things and heard voices her whole life. A lot of it stopped when she met your father and stayed on her medication steady,"

"What made you come to the house that day?" Brandon asked. He stared down at the dock as if it were the only thing in the world. The splintered wood was an anchor and it was the only thing stopping him from spiraling away.

"It didn't take long for her to start backsliding after your father died and I was worried about you?"

"So you knew she was dangerous because of her illness?"

"Son mentally ill doesn't equal dangerous. Everyone is different but your mom had tendencies. She always said she heard voices that told her to do terrible things," his uncle said, and took another drink of his beer. He scratched at his salt and pepper beard and stared across the water. Brandon saw the pain on his face. This was the first time his uncle had talked about his sister at length.

"So when I came to live with you. It wasn't so mom could get better after my dad's death was it?"

"No. She attempted to kill you. She spent the next ten years in a psych ward. Your mom's life was hard I'm just glad she's at peace now," he said.

"Yeah she certainly seems better," Brandon said. If he ignored the fact that she went out of her way every day to belittle him or drive him crazy in some other way. He looked at the water and remembered Sarah's face and the other woman with no skin and worried they might actually be waiting for him beneath the surface of the brown water where he couldn't see. A chill shot down his spine.

"What do you mean?" His uncle asked.

"Well other than still not being able to move around too good she seems fine otherwise," Brandon said. His uncle sat his empty beer bottle down on the dock a mixture of confusion and worry etched on his face.

"Brandon are you off your meds?" He asked.

"I was for a little bit but back on for two weeks straight as of this morning,"

"Brandon your mother died in the fire. Jennifer too. Don't you remember?" His uncle asked. Brandon smiled and shook his head.

"No. That's not right," he said. Why was his uncle messing with him? It had to be some kind of cruel joke. He couldn't remember his uncle ever being cruel before and it troubled him.

"Oh my God. Their bodies going missing. Was that you?"

"What are you talking about!" Brandon shot out of his lawn chair and stared at his uncle. Rage boiled inside him and screamed to be let out. He clenched his fists and his uncle got to his feet.

"Why would you say these things?" Brandon asked and stalked away from the dock.

"Brandon I think it would be a good idea if you stayed here," his uncle said and came after him putting a hand on his shoulder. Brandon wheeled around and his uncle shrank from him.

"Don't touch me. I have to go," he said. Brandon ran across the backyard leaving the dock and his uncle behind. His uncle didn't try to stop him again.

—TWELVE—

Brandon sped home along the backroads with gritted teeth and a death grip on his steering wheel. There was no way what his uncle said could be true. He replayed the night of the fire in his head over and over again. How he came home to find the apartment on fire. How he had managed to pull Jennifer out just before the firefighters arrived. His mother couldn't have died in the fire because she didn't even live with them.

A second set of memories tried to push their way forward as he drove. The road in front of him disappeared, replaced by a vision of Jennifer covered in blackened skin. He crinkled his nose as he recalled the smell of burnt flesh.

"No. It's not true!" Brandon screamed and punched the steering wheel with both hands.

He slid into the driveway not slowing enough to take the turn. He threw the car in park and jumped out before running in the house.

The dark, quiet house greeted him. No blue light from the television illuminated the walls in the living room. No voices of screeching pastors rattled from the speakers. He found nothing but oppressive silence. Brandon walked into the living room and went weak in the knees. The blackened television sat against the wall. Across from the television sat the hospital bed and on the bed laid his mother.

Her powder blue night gown hung loosely on the thin frame of her corpse. Sections of her skull peeked at him around the blackened, burnt sections of flesh on her face. Wisps of hair laid against her head in the spots where her hair hadn't completely burned away. Brandon staggered backward and fell against the wall. His heart hammered in his chest and his mouth went dry. He slid back along the wall not trusting his legs to keep him up and backed out of the room.

Brandon bent over and rested his arms on his knees while he looked down at the kitchen floor through watering eyes. This couldn't be true, it couldn't be. He talked to his mother every day. When was the last time he talked to her? The day he started being stringent about taking his medication. *No, she was quiet that day you looked in on her she was asleep.* Was she though? He questioned himself. He looked up and saw the basement door on the other side of the kitchen, and his stomach dropped. Ice cold dread seeped into every bone of his body. He needed to go downstairs and see Jennifer, he had to be sure, while another part of him never wanted to go through that door or down those stairs again.

He stood up and took an unsteady step toward the basement door and bile rose in his throat. He knew what he was going to find down there, memories of the fire were coming back. Brandon remembered being called to Jerry's office and being told there was a fire at home. He rushed home to find the firefighters putting out the fire. He watched the coroner and EMS bring both body bags out of the wet, still smoldering building while he talked to the police.

The following days were dark. He stopped medicating and spent them among the blackened ruins taking anything salvageable which wasn't much. He took the two televisions. His mother and Jennifer would both need them when they got home he convinced himself.

The first step to the basement creaked under Brandon's weight and he remembered taking the bodies from the funeral home in the middle of the night. He brought them both back to his childhood home where his mother had lived until he brought her to the apartment to take care of her and the three of them got back to their life. They hadn't died, it had just been a real close call is all.

He reached the bottom of the stairs and took in the room he had really been living in for the last few months. The ratty mattress singed with burn marks on the floor. The television across from the bed with the shattered screen. There had never been any movies. His stomach tied itself in knots and his mouth watered. The vomit wanted to come but he fought it down until he found Jennifer.

Jennifer's burnt corpse sat in the lawn chair next to the mattress facing the broken television. Strips of skin were sewn onto her body everywhere in a hodge podge pattern. She looked like the world's most grotesque quilt. He could see the truth of it now and it hit him like a ton of bricks. She had been dead for months. There had been no arguments. She hadn't asked him for skin. He had killed those two women for no reason at all. He hit the floor on all fours and wretched. When he finished vomiting he looked at Jennifer's effigy of dead skin and wailed. What had he done? If nothing had been real then he doubted the monstrous faces with the missing eyes and mouths of flies had been real either. There had been nothing wrong with those women and he had killed them. His hands shook as he pushed himself up off the floor, his mind racing. He had to get rid of it all. Luckily, the women's bodies were already gone but his mother and Jennifer had to go too. He didn't have time for a normal burial. Tonight he would put the two of them in the river just like he had the other two. Once that was done he would join them because it turned out after all this time the only monster that had truly existed and needed killing was himself.

—THIRTEEN—

Genevieve sat at her desk pouring over the photos from the nightclub and tried get the vision of the skinless woman wrapped in plastic out of her mind. She had seen the skinned woman in her dreams. She came to Genevieve in her bedroom, her bloody exposed muscles dripping a mixture of blood and dirty river water on the carpet. The woman tried to tell Genevieve who killed her but without lips she couldn't enunciate her words.

"Hey," Clive said, and Genevieve jumped in her seat. She was no longer in her bedroom but back at her desk. She must have dozed off. She gathered the photos from the nightclub up into a single, neat pile and rubbed her eyes.

"You alright," he asked.

"Yeah. Didn't get a lot of sleep last night," she said.

"I come with good news," Clive said, and sat down on the corner of her desk. He rubbed her shoulder and the warmth from his hand spread through her. She looked at him and saw kindness in his eyes. He was worried about her he didn't have to say it. Beneath his gruff exterior Clive was a good guy and it was one of the things that had attracted her to him in the first place.

"What do you got?" She asked.

"Meet Brandon Ross," Clive said and put a paper down on her desk. On the paper was a picture of his driver's license.

"But wait, there's more. Take a look at this," he said and dropped another paper on her desk. Genevieve picked it up and read it over.

"Wait. Is this real life?" She asked. The paperwork was a police report from a funeral home in McDonald, PA. Two dead bodies had gone missing in the middle of the night four months ago now. The bodies of Brandon's mother and girlfriend.

"Did anybody talk to him?" She asked.

"Nope. Sheriff did a follow-up with a Stephen Ross. That would be Brandon's uncle. Brandon however, had disappeared," Clive said. Genevieve sat back in her chair and looked at the ceiling. She let out an exasperated sigh. Sometimes the complete ineptitude of the people in her profession flabbergasted her.

"So I'm assuming the address on the license is no good?" She asked.

"No. It's the address of the apartment that burned down," he said.

"Do we have an address on the uncle?" Clive pulled a piece of paper out of his pocket and handed it to her with a wink. It had an address written on it in his barely legible scrawl.

"Ready when you are?" He said.

A half an hour after meeting with Brandon's uncle, Clive and Genevieve pulled into the parking lot of the plant on West Carson Street. He guided the car into one of the visitor's parking spaces and turned it off with another backfire.

"We should have brought my car," Genevieve said.

"Again, Why do you insist on disrespecting my girl like this? It's alright she didn't mean it," he said, and stroked the dashboard lovingly.

According to the uncle the last place of employment he knew of for Brandon was Allied Security here at the plant. Stephen had given them a lot of other information too, none of it good. According to the uncle Brandon was sick and had said some very troubling things the last time they spoke. The more Stephen told them the more Genevieve was convinced Brandon was their man.

They exited the car and were immediately greeted by a small, wiry man wearing a black jacket with the words Allied Security over the chest pocket in silver, capital letters.

"Good morning. Something I can help you with?" He asked and both Clive and Genevieve flashed their badges.

"As a matter of fact there is. We need to speak with your boss," Clive said.

"Right this way," the man said and lead them across the parking lot with no further questions.

The man, Hiram was his name, she learned lead them down to the basement and down the long white hallway where an office set at the end before the hall turned left. Genevieve and Clive tried to whisper amongst themselves but their voices carried in the empty hallway.

"Is Brandon in some kind of trouble?" Hiram asked.

"Do you know Brandon?" Genevieve asked dodging the question.

"A little. He tends to keep to himself but he seems like an alright guy," he said. They came to a stop at the door and Hiram knocked before sticking his head in.

"Hey Jerry, I have the police out here. Something about Brandon. They want to talk to you," he said.

The first thing Genevieve noticed about Jerry was his size as he struggled to get up from the chair behind his desk. He planted his hands against the edge of the desk and winced.

"Sorry back problems. Jerry Offerman how can I help you?" He asked and stuck out his hand. Both Genevieve and Clive shook it.

"Detectives Bosco and Wurtz," Clive said, and they both showed their badges. Jerry made a show of looking at them as he lowered himself back into his seat.

"We were hoping we could talk to one of your employees. Brandon Ross. Is he here?" Genevieve asked and put the picture of him from the nightclub down on Jerry's desk. He gave it a cursory look.

"I'd love to help but Brandon hasn't been to work in a couple of days," he said.

"Do you have a current address for him on file?" Clive asked. Jerry pulled himself up out of his seat again and made his way across the office toward the silver file cabinet in the corner. Genevieve watched him finger through the files before pulling out the one he was looking for. She had a feeling they were wasting their time. The file was going to have the same address as the driver's license and the one the uncle had given them. An address that lead to nothing but a burnt down building. Somehow this guy was a ghost. A moment later her suspicions were confirmed when Jerry read off the same address.

"That's the place that burned down. You know I don't think he ever gave me an updated address after that," he said.

"Is there anyone here he's close with?" Genevieve asked.

"Go get me Lucy," Jerry said, and Hiram nodded before leaving the room. Genevieve looked at the nightclub picture again before refolding it and putting it back in her pocket. She hoped this Lucy could give them something to go on because if she couldn't they were looking at an impasse and she really didn't want to be called to another waterlogged body on a riverbank.

Twenty minutes later they were in the empty break room with the aforementioned Lucy. She sat on one side of a table while they sat on the other. Genevieve knew they might be on track. Lucy kept wringing her hands and looking everywhere but at them.

"I understand you're close with Brandon Ross?" Genevieve asked.

"Has something happened to him? He hasn't been to work in a couple of days and I can't seem to get ahold of him," Lucy said.

"How well do you know him?" Clive asked.

"Well we've been dating for about a month,"

"Have you ever been to his place?" Genevieve asked picking up the baton from her partner.

"No. On our first date we went into the city and the second time he came to my place. Though he did say he lived in Crafton. What's this about?" Lucy asked.

"Are you aware of the two murders. The two bodies pulled out of the river?" Clive asked.

"A little," she said and stopped. "Wait surely you don't think Brandon did it?" She asked.

"Were you aware his mother and girlfriend were killed in a fire and that their bodies went missing?" Genevieve asked and watched Lucy's face as she tried to process the information.

"They didn't die. He told me his girlfriend was badly burned," Lucy said and Genevieve got a sick feeling in her stomach. She hoped she was wrong but she suspected he killed the girls and took their skin for the corpse of his dead girlfriend.

"Did he ever tell you where in Crafton he lived?" Clive asked.

"No," Lucy said, tears streamed from her eyes and Genevieve passed her a tissue from her pocket. She always carried some on hand starting in the spring because seasonal allergies kicked her ass.

"But on our first date he took me somewhere he said he likes to go when he needs to think," Lucy said.

"Can you tell us where?" Genevieve asked.

"Only if you take me with you. I have to hear it from him," Lucy said.

—FOURTEEN—

Lucy's mind raced and her stomach tied itself in knots as Clive guided the little blue car up Grandview Avenue toward the lookout Brandon had taken her to on their first date.

The sun had begun to drop toward the horizon painting the old brick buildings in this part of town in blazing orange light. The car's engine bogged down and part of her worried they might not make it up the hill. The engine backfired with a loud bang and they managed to pick up a little speed for a couple of seconds before bogging down again. No matter how she played it over in her head Lucy couldn't believe what they were saying about Brandon. He was a sweet, kindhearted man. There was no way he could be a killer and definitely no way he could have completely skinned a woman the way the second body had been found. She refused to believe it. This all had to be a misunderstanding.

"If he's there let me talk to him first okay?" Lucy asked.

"I don't know if that is a good idea. He's dangerous," Genevieve said.

"If he wanted to hurt me he's had plenty of chances. I won't do anything stupid," she said. She kept replaying her mother's last days in her mind. How she had needed help and Lucy failed to save her. She didn't want it to happen again. If Brandon did do these things then he needed help and she wasn't going to fail again.

"Alright but the first sign of trouble you're done," Genevieve said, and Lucy nodded.

"I got it,"

Clive pulled the little blue car against the curb on the opposite side of the street from the lookout and the three of them climbed out. People passed by the lookout going in both directions but only one person was on it. They leaned against the railing looking out over the city and even though Lucy couldn't see his face she knew it was Brandon. Genevieve nodded to Clive and he hung back at the entrance.

"I need everyone to get away," he said keeping his voice low and guided pedestrians away from the entrance. Genevieve and Lucy continued on. They took a few steps closer before Genevieve put a hand on her shoulder and pointed at the ground. Haphazard droplets and streaks of blood made the sidewalk leading to the overlook look like a Jackson Pollock painting. She pulled her pistol with the other hand and held Lucy in place while she assessed the situation.

"It's okay I'm not going to hurt anybody else," Brandon said from his spot at the railing and Lucy's mind went into a tailspin as those words echoed around inside her head. *I'm not going to hurt anybody else.* What they were saying was true. He had killed those women.

"Brandon what's going on?" Lucy asked when she found her voice.

"I messed up bad," he said

"You killed those women?" She asked.

"I did," he said and his voice broke. She wanted to go to him but she knew Genevieve would never allow it.

"I was off my meds. I stopped taking them after my mother and Jennifer died and after a while I forgot I wasn't taking them as far as I knew I was only missing a dose here and there. I started seeing things. They were alive again I talked to them both everyday but Jennifer was so burned and I wasn't home when the fire started so I had to make it better for her. I killed them and I took their skin," he said. Hot bile rose in her throat and she did everything she could to keep it in. She took a couple of deep breaths and didn't speak again until she was sure she could do it without vomiting.

"So what changed? What are we doing up here?" She asked.

"You happened. You made me want to get serious about my medication again. Two days ago I hit two weeks straight and everything came back. I remembered they had been dead the whole time and that I killed two women for no reason but it's ok. I'm making it right," he said and turned from the rail to face them for the first time.

"Jesus Christ," Genevieve said, and lowered her gun. Lucy's knees went weak and she dropped on the concrete. Brandon's face was gone. He had peeled it off himself. All that was left beneath his hair was his muscles, eyes, and teeth. Suddenly the blood patterns on the concrete made sense.

"I took their skin so I gave up some of mine," he said.

"Brandon you seem remorseful. Why don't you come with us? You need medical attention," Genevieve said.

119

"No. What I need is to make things even. My mom was mad and she passed her madness on to me. I'm going to break the chain here and now," he said, and looked at Lucy.

"I wish I had met you five months ago," he said.

"Please don't do this," Lucy said, and Brandon smiled at her.

"I'm not your mother. This isn't your fault," he said, and before she could move or say anything he let himself fall backward over the railing and disappeared from sight. Lucy wanted to cry, she wanted to scream, she wanted to get up and run for the railing but she did nothing. It was as if her body had turned against her and shut down. No matter what he said she felt like she failed to save someone she loved again.

Brandon looked at the sky as he fell backward and tried to keep an image of Lucy in his mind as he fell. Pain exploded in his head and shoulders as he landed headfirst on the hillside and started tumbling backward. He flipped and rolled over and over again bouncing off of rocks and branches as he continued his descent.

He hit the bottom and struck the back of his head off the iron rail of the train tracks and things went fuzzy. He knew he was dying and it was ok because soon it would all be over; the monster would be dead. He relaxed and turned his head to the side where he saw Sarah and the dead skinned woman. They nodded at him and he offered a faint smile in return. Now that the time was here he found he wasn't afraid to die. He enjoyed the first true moments of silence he had in months and thought of Lucy as everything faded to black.

WRITING PLAYLIST

My Only Enemy – American Hi-Fi
Something In The Way – Nirvana
Opposite – Biffy Clyro
Found Out About You – Gin Blossoms
Prayers For Rain – The Cure
X&Y – Coldplay
The Quiet Things That No One Ever Knows – Brand New
Littlething – Jimmy Eat World
Silver and Cold – AFI
Possum Kingdom – The Toadies
Losing My Religion – R.E.M.
This Love – Taylor Swift
Officially Dead – Veruca Salt
Wall Of Sound – American Hi-Fi

ABOUT THE AUTHOR

Matthew Standiford (he/him) fell in love with horror and knew he wanted to be a writer the moment he read The Shining in 6th grade. He is a married father of four, and retired United States Army Veteran. This is his first novella. For more information please follow @mattstandiford on Twitter

Printed in Great Britain
by Amazon